"I'll do anything you want,"
Molly pleaded.

"No," Garrett said.

"I want to stay here," she persisted. "I'll be your cook, your housekeeper...anything."

As Garrett's heated gaze moved over her body, Molly's defiance died, and awareness grew in its stead. She could see the hunger in his eyes.

"Anything?" he asked.

She swallowed hard. Her bravado nearly crumbled; shame coursed through her. Then she remembered that this place was the only home she'd ever known. Her chin climbed a degree higher. "Anything," she said, her voice a wisp of sound.

Dear Reader,

Welcome to the Silhouette **Special Edition** experience! With your search for consistently satisfying reading in mind, every month the authors and editors of Silhouette **Special Edition** aim to offer you a stimulating blend of deep emotions and high romance.

The name Silhouette **Special Edition** and the distinctive arch on the cover represent a commitment—a commitment to bring you six sensitive, substantial novels each month. In the pages of a Silhouette **Special Edition**, compelling true-to-life characters face riveting emotional issues—and come out winners. All the authors in the series strive for depth, vividness and warmth in writing these stories of living and loving in today's world.

The result, we hope, is romance you can believe in. Deeply emotional, richly romantic, infinitely rewarding—that's the Silhouette **Special Edition** experience. Come share it with us—six times a month! With this month's distinguished roster of gifted contemporary writers—Bay Matthews, Karen Keast, Barbara Faith, Madelyn Dohrn, Dawn Flindt and Andrea Edwards—you won't want to miss a single volume.

Best wishes,

Leslie Kazanjian,
Senior Editor

BAY MATTHEWS
Laughter on the Wind

Silhouette Special Edition

Published by Silhouette Books New York

America's Publisher of Contemporary Romance

For Mom—
sounding board, slave driver,
cheerleader and unpaid PR person.
Thanks for believing in me.
I love you.

SILHOUETTE BOOKS
300 East 42nd St., New York, N.Y. 10017

BAY MATTHEWS

of Haughton, Louisiana, describes herself as a dreamer and an incurable romantic. Married at an early age to her high school sweetheart, she claims she grew up with her three children. Now that only the youngest is at home, writing romances adds a new dimension to the already exciting life she leads on her husband's Thoroughbred farm.

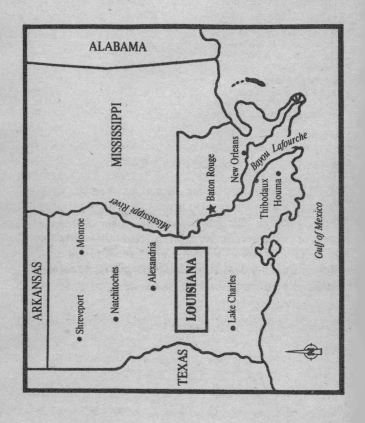

Chapter One

I'm sorry, Molly, but all I can give you is thirty days to come up with the money.''

The memory of the banker's words danced through Molly O'Connell's mind like the lazy Louisiana wind danced through the wind chimes hanging from the second-floor gallery.

"Thirty days or sell out. What do you think of that, Silvie?"

Slouched in a white wicker chaise longue with a forgotten glass of lemonade in her hand, Molly was alone, yet she asked the question aloud, as if she expected Silvie, the ghost who reputedly haunted the one-hundred-and-fifty-year-old plantation house, to answer. Molly looked up at the hundreds of tiny bells that comprised the wind chimes while she waited for an answer. "Well? Are you going to answer me or not?".

There was barely any movement from the bells. The sultry early-June breeze was supposed to carry Silvie's laughter, but today the desultory chiming sounded as forlorn as Molly felt.

"You can't believe it, either, huh?" she said, taking the lethargic sound as Silvie's answer.

When Molly had come to the house as a shy four-teen-year-old and heard the legend of Silvia Antilly, she had latched onto the idea of Silvie with unaccountable fervor. Growing up, Molly had felt overshadowed by her flamboyant mother and outgoing sister. Often left alone, Molly had quickly adopted Silvie as friend and confidante, someone she could talk to when there was no one else.

She'd longed to hear the tinkling, childlike laughter of the resident ghost, and when she finally did—or fancied she did—it reminded her of the sound of tinkling bells. It was Molly's idea to buy the chimes, so she could "fake out" her friends who came to sleep over, and there had been bell chimes on the upper gallery of Rambler's Rest ever since.

Today, Silvie was being no help. Molly sighed and took a sip of her watery lemonade. The bank had been very gracious to work with her for the past three years while she scraped and scrimped and still grew further and further behind repaying the mortgage—a legacy she'd inherited along with the house. The note was considerable, money her mother had borrowed against the house to maintain her extravagant life-style in Europe, a life-style that included the skiing accident that had cost her life.

Now it appeared that Molly had borrowed all the time she could. She was faced with two options. Macdonald Henning, president of the bank, had a buyer for the place, and if she chose to sell, she could not only get out from under the burden of payments, she would have a decent sum of money to start over with. The other option was to come up with the back payments...in thirty days. The money she owed was more than she earned in four months of teaching Louisiana history at the junior high school in nearby Houma.

Henning had urged her to sell, pointing out that the buyer was being very generous. It was a miracle anyone wanted to buy the place with the economy in such a depressed state. Fighting her own state of depression, Molly shifted her gaze to the peeling, aqua-tinted boards of the gallery ceiling and realized that she couldn't put off a paint job much longer.

As it often did lately, despair settled over her. It was always something. If she wasn't saving money to have the foundation stabilized or to mortar loose bricks, she was using it to repair the intricate plasterwork of the ceilings or to re-putty the windows. Her hand tightened around the sweating glass, and she squeezed her eyes shut, as if by blocking out reality, she could somehow make the necessity of painting the exterior of the house and paying the past-due bank note disappear. Unfortunately, it didn't work.

She swung her bare feet to the wooden floor and stood, leaning against the waist-high railing and fighting the urge to give in to the threatening sting of tears. Clinging to the smooth, round support post with one hand, she lifted the other and pressed the glass of lemonade to her throbbing temple.

Her anguished gaze swept the three-acre front lawn. A driveway of crushed white shells was bordered on both sides by peeling, multi-trunked crape myrtles. A thick bank of azaleas cut a horseshoe-shaped swath through the thick green carpet of St. Augustine. Brick pillars with a lion rampant on top and clumps of emerald-hued Pampas grass flanked each entrance of the driveway. A wrought-iron fence, festooned with masses of wild roses, stretched along the front of the lawn.

Years of watching the seasons change her beloved landscape had taught Molly that the azaleas became a sea of pink and white blossoms in the spring and that the roses would soon be a riot of tiny pink flowers. The heat of summer would explode the tips of the crape myrtles into frilly, mauve blossoms, and the Pampas grass would sprout feathery off-white plumes that reminded her of horses' tails.

Beyond the yard was the secondary highway that divided the plantation's two-hundred acres. Once noted for producing quality sugar, the fields had lain barren since plummeting sugar prices made the effort to produce a crop more trouble than it was worth, putting a stop to the plantation's main source of income.

It hurt to think of the wasted land, but she had neither the knowledge nor the capital to figure out how to put it to a new, productive use. Instead, she paid to have the grass bush hogged every summer and kept the fences in repair—the bare minimum of upkeep.

Molly chewed her bottom lip. What was she going to do? She couldn't let the bank take this place. She couldn't. Maybe she could ask her father.... No. Ian O'Connell was putting two other children through college. He had his own financial burdens. Her fingertips caressed the painted surface of the wooden post, and she brought the glass to her lips, hoping the cool drink would ease the aching fullness in her throat.

Blinking rapidly, she turned to go back into the house, trying to ignore the fact that the screen on the double doors needed replacing. She swung the door wide open and let it slam behind her, heading toward the upstairs bathroom. She hoped the aspirin in the medicine chest would offer relief.

Her bare feet whispered across the plank floors, which were smooth from years of wear. Hewn from the resined core of the plentiful Louisiana pine trees, the floors were naturally resistant to decay and insects. They had even withstood the ravages of over one-hundred-and-fifty years of living and the desecration of Yankee soldiers who had used the house as a bivouac during the Civil War.

To Molly, the floors were the very heart and foundation of the house. And, if the floors were the heart and foundation of the house, the house was the heart and foundation of her very being, even though maintaining the old home and the surrounding acreage was, like the bank note, a burden.

She'd never minded.

Rambler's Rest was home.

And had been since her mother had come to the plantation as the new bride of Jonathan Garrett Rambler....

Molly sat next to her older sister, Krystal, in the back seat of the '77 Buick and wrung her hands in nervous excitement. The sound of her mother's and sister's light chatter, punctuated by an occasional deep-toned comment from Jon, was a muted background for her chaotic thoughts.

They were moving again, and Molly was about to embark on another major change in her life. She should be used to moving by now, but she didn't thrive on change in the same way as her mother and her sister.

Liz and Jon Rambler had recently returned from Hawaii, where they'd gone to honeymoon after their wedding over three weeks ago. Jon had spent the last few days helping them pack up their belongings in preparation for moving into his home, a plantation house he called Rambler's Rest.

It was apparent, even to Molly, that Jon, who made no apologies for the failure of his three previous marriages and had eluded the matrimonial "trap" for an unprecedented ten years, had fallen hard for her mother. So hard, in fact, that in order to spend more time with Liz, he had decided to turn over the everyday management of the plantation to his son, Garrett, who had recently received a degree in agriculture from LSU Baton Rouge.

Molly was a bit worried about how Jon's children would accept her and Krystal. He had only two children from his three marriages—Garrett, born of his first marriage, and a nineteen-year-old daughter, Shiloh, born of the second. Meeting Shiloh was not an issue at present, since she lived with her mother in Tennessee, but Garrett, who had chosen to live with his father when he was sixteen, would be making his home with them.

At least her mother seemed happy... for now anyway, and that was a blessing. Liz was always happy when there was a new man in her life, especially if that man was handsome and had a great deal of money, like Jon. And when Liz was happy, life was much easier for everyone.

Unfortunately, most of the men weren't so nice. Somehow, Liz seemed to attract the wrong kind—the loud braggarts who didn't particularly like teenagers around. Jon Rambler was an exception. Warm, funny, and generous to a fault, he and Molly had hit it off from the start, and she was glad her mother had married him.

"You're awfully quiet, Molly," Jon said, the sound of his pleasant voice interrupting her thoughts.

Her eyes flew open, meeting his in the rearview mirror. Jon smiled, and crinkles appeared at the corners of his eyes. Molly couldn't resist smiling back.

"I'm scared," she confessed.

"Scared? Why? Did someone already tell you about Silvie?"

Molly's eyebrows drew together in a frown. "Silvie? Who's she?"

"Jon…" Liz cautioned, casting a reproachful look in his direction. "Don't fill her head with that nonsense. She's fanciful enough as it is."

Jon laughed and brought his bride's hand to his lips. "Molly isn't fanciful. Of the three of you, she's the only one with her feet on the ground." The statement was made in a teasing way, but Molly didn't miss the flash of fire in her mother's eyes or the almost imperceptible tightening of her lips.

Molly stifled a smile. Always needing to be the center of her man's universe, Liz was angry because Jon was showing attention to Molly, not her. Molly knew what an effort it must be for her mother to control her anger, but she managed to, which meant that Molly could indulge in trying to satisfy her natural curiosity for historical stories.

"Who's Silvie?" she asked again.

"She's the ghost who lives at Rambler's Rest."

"Ghost!"

"Hmpf!" Krystal's snort of disbelief collided with Molly's shocked exclamation.

"Ghost," Jon said with a nod. "No self-respecting plantation is without at least one ghost. Ours is Silvia Marie Antilly, or Silvie, as everyone called her. She was the younger sister of Lisette Antilly, whose father built the house. Back, then, it was called Belle Maison."

"How did it get the name Rambler's Rest?" Molly asked.

"Patience, patience," Jon said. "I'm getting there. Lisette's father died, and her mother—" he smiled at Liz "—another Elizabeth, married a handsome rogue named Henri Duschene. Henri, the no-account bastard, slowly poisoned Elizabeth with arsenic just to get the plantation. After Elizabeth died, Silvie, who was about sixteen and full of mischief, decided that she wanted to marry Henri and become the mistress of the plantation."

"She wanted to marry her stepfather?" Krystal interrupted. "Wouldn't he be *old*?"

"He was around thirty-five," Jon explained, "and it wasn't uncommon to have a wide disparity of ages back then. Anyway, she decided to pursue him, and she did. Trouble was, Henri was way out of her league. She got *enceinte*."

"*Enceinte?*" Krystal said.

"Pregnant," Molly supplied, loftily, having just finished a year of French.

"How disgusting," Krystal murmured.

"What did Silvie do?" Molly asked, resting her forearms on the back of Jon's seat and speaking almost directly into his ear.

"She told Lisette, who advised her to tell Henri. Lisette supposed he would do the honorable thing and marry Silvie, but she thought wrong. Henri refused. He and Silvie got into a terrible fight. Lisette heard the commotion at the top of the stairs. She grabbed a heavy candlestick, and when she tried to help Silvie get away, Henri turned on her. Lisette begged for help, but Silvie must have been too frightened to do anything. She just stood there and watched Henri choke the life out of her sister. Desperate, Lisette began to strike Henri with the candlestick. She got in a good blow, and he fell down the stairs.''

"Wow!" Molly breathed, captivated by the story. "What happened next?"

"The girls' mammy told them to run, and they did. They thought Henri was dead, you see, but he wasn't. Silvie went to New Orleans, but Lisette was right under his nose at a neighboring plantation, masquerading as a nun and teaching some orphaned children my ancestor Nate Rambler had sort of inherited."

"How?"

"That's another story, Molly," Jon teased.

Molly's sigh mirrored her disappointment. It was all so fascinating!

"As soon as Henri had sufficiently recovered, he started looking for the girls. He wanted them both dead for what they'd done. Lisette wanted to find Silvie, too, so she and Nate went to New Orleans to look for her."

"How did they know to go to New Orleans?"

"Lisette had told Silvie to go there and stay with the Ursuline nuns. She did find Silvie, but she was sick and her baby was due at any time. Before Lisette and Nate could take her back to Nate's plantation, Henri's men recognized Lisette and kidnapped her. They brought her back to Belle Maison, where Henri tried to poison her. Thank goodness one of the cats got the stuff instead, or I wouldn't be here telling you this story,'' Jon said.

Molly giggled.

"While this was all going on, Nate brought Silvie back. Silvie knew she owed it to her sister to help her. After all, Lisette had saved her life once. So, even though Silvie was sick and there was a storm brewing, she got in a buggy and drove to Belle Maison, intending to kill Henri for what he'd done to her family. When Nate found out that Silvie was gone, he followed and met up with Lisette, who had managed to escape.

"They rode through the storm to Belle Maison and got there in time to see Silvie and Henri struggling on the upper gallery. Silvie was screaming over the sound of the wind, and as they dismounted they saw Henri pitch Silvie over the railing. Then he leaned over, and they say there was a wicked smile on his face for just a moment before the railing gave way, killing him, too."

The breath Molly had been holding trickled from her in relief. Thank goodness Henri had gotten what he deserved. "What happened to Lisette?"

"Lisette and Nate were married soon after that," Jon said, "and they changed Belle Maison's name to Rambler's Rest. And that's how the Ramblers came to be here."

"What about Silvie?" Molly asked. "What about her ghost?"

Jon's eyes smiled into hers. "They say that soon after her death, whenever the wind blew, they could hear her laughter—not the wild, crazy laughter they heard from the gallery the day she died—but the happy laughter of her childhood. Legend says that her ghost will continue to haunt the house until she can somehow repay the debt she owes Lisette for saving her life. Only then will she find her own rest."

Molly smiled in contentment. "That's a great story, Jon." She paused, as if she was afraid to speak. "Have you ever heard her laughing?" she asked at last.

The look in Jon's eyes was serious. "Every now and then, Molly, I swear I do," he said. And Molly believed him, though she saw the skeptical shake of her mother's head.

"How much farther?" Liz asked, drawing her husband's attention back to her.

"Down the road about two miles."

The next few minutes passed quickly for Molly. Wrapped in the haze of pleasure left over from the tale Jon had just told her, Molly sat with her eyes closed and her head resting against the back of the seat.

"We're here."

There was no mistaking the pride and excitement in Jon's voice. Molly's eyes flew open. Pushing herself into a sitting position, she peered through the gathering twilight at the house they were approaching.

Rambler's Rest stood on a slight knoll, its two-and-a-half stories climbing stoically toward the darkening sky. Molly's hungry gaze moved from the lower floor to the second-story gallery from which Silvie and Henri had fallen to their deaths.

Her heart began to tap out a rapid rhythm. Rambler's Rest wasn't fancy like many of the plantation houses she had seen in books. It was a plain white wooden house with dark-green shutters and six stolid pillars that supported the two galleries spanning the front of the house. Something about the house said "permanence" to her. Perhaps, she mused, it was because there wasn't anything too grand about it. And then again, perhaps it was the fact that the house had been there for a hundred and fifty years and looked as if it would be there for a hundred and fifty more.

Whatever it was, she knew without a doubt that she had finally come home . . . and that if it was at all possible, she was never, never going to leave. . . .

A loud ringing roused Molly from a deep sleep. Hoping to quiet the clatter, she slapped the back of the old-fashioned alarm clock. The ringing persisted. Finally, the fact that it was the phone, not the clock, registered. She dragged the receiver to her ear. "Hello."

"Molly?"

Though there was considerable static on the line and the single word sounded as though it were being spoken from the bottom of a deep well, there was no disguising the caller's identity. Molly stifled a groan. Krystal.

"Molly, are you there?"

Molly pushed herself up on her elbow. She really wasn't anxious to hear about her sister's latest problem. And a problem it would undoubtedly be. Krystal drew trouble like flowers drew honeybees.

"Yeah, I'm here," Molly said, urging some false enthusiasm into her voice. "How are you, Krys?"

"Fine. Well, not so fine, actually. Freddy and I are in Greece," Krystal said, referring to her latest—her third—husband.

Molly fought back a scathing retort. Here she was trying to keep a roof over her head while Krystal sashayed around Greece! "Greece," Molly said through clenched teeth. "How nice!"

"Yeah, we were having a really good time until we ran into Spiro."

Molly's eyebrows lifted in surprise. Spiro had been Krystal's second husband. Their marriage had been brief and tempestuous, lasting only until the handsome young Greek had fallen under Liz's spell. The subsequent divorce wasn't pleasant. Spiro and Liz had married soon after, and the rift between Liz and her older daughter lasted until the day she died.

"Spiro? Good grief! What happened?" Molly asked.

"I think I still love him," Krystal confessed.

Molly's eyes drifted shut in disbelief as she sank back against the pillow. Love. She doubted Krystal could spell the word, much less have any idea of what it meant. "You still have the hots for him, right?"

Krystal's laughter was low and suggestive. "Yeah. I still have the hots for him, but I ought to make him a eunuch. Can you imagine him preferring Liz to me?"

Molly wasn't touching that with a ten-foot pole. "I plead the fifth," she said. "So are you dumping Freddy to take Spiro back or what?"

"Not exactly," Krystal said.

Molly heard the hesitancy in her sister's voice. "Then what? Do you mind spitting it out? This is costing money, and I know you've charged it to my account."

Krystal laughed. "Money's made to be spent, Molly, and life's to enjoy."

Molly's mouth tightened. "Right."

A sigh drifted through the phone lines. "Freddy caught Spiro and me in what he thought was a compromising situation."

"What he *thought* was a compromising situation?" Molly pressed.

"Spiro was kissing me. I wasn't kissing him," Krystal explained. "The bastard," she tacked on.

"I thought you said you still wanted him."

"I do. He's undoubtedly the best lover I've ever had, but I'm not going to let him know that the first time we're together...not after the way he treated me."

"So what are you going to do about Freddy?"

"I still want to be married to him, of course. He may be broke, but he does have a title."

Molly rubbed at the double lines between her eyebrows. "But you'd sleep with Spiro?"

"In a heartbeat."

Krystal's duplicity was too much for Molly. Her voice was laced with bitterness. "Give yourself some time. You'll think of some way to bring Freddy to heel.''

"Yeah. Maybe you're right," Krystal said. "So, how's it going with you?"

Terrible, sister dear. "Not bad," Molly lied. She was never tempted to spill her guts to Krystal.

"Money's tight there, too, huh?"

"How did you know?"

"I lived there for a while, remember? That place would drain Onassis. You know what you need to do, darlin'?" Krystal drawled.

"What's that?"

"Sell the jewelry or those damned pictures if you haven't already."

The very thought horrified Molly. Nate Rambler had bought the jewelry for Lisette. The paintings were a Landseer that Nate's family had sent at the birth of Lisette's first-born son and a little-known work by Rosa Bonheur that Nate had bought his bride when they toured France after the war.

"I couldn't do that," Molly told her sister firmly. "Those things are priceless. They've been in the Rambler family for years."

Krystal tsked-tsked. "Then you're gonna have to find yourself a sugar daddy to take care of you and that drafty old house," she suggested in honeyed tones.

Molly sighed. Finding a man seemed to be Krystal's answer to every problem.

"I'll keep it in mind."

"Do that. Uh-oh. Here comes Freddy," Krystal said breathlessly. "I've gotta go. I'll call you soon, okay?"

"Sure," Molly said. "G'bye."

She heard the faint click as Krystal hung up. Though the laws of nature demanded that Molly love her sister, she didn't particularly like her. Neither her mother nor her sister had endearing qualities to her way of thinking. They were both too competitive, too self-serving, too materialistic. And their moral code was almost non-existent, as Krystal's current situation with Spiro and Freddy proved.

Molly wondered what would have happened if she'd been like them—if she'd been irresponsible and flighty instead of solid and dependable. Would it have mattered? Would Liz have taken on a more motherly role if Molly hadn't? Had she, in fact, aided and abetted her mother's and sister's helplessness by always taking it on herself to do things for them?

No, she decided with a sideways glance at the phone and a final shake of her head. She hadn't wanted the role of caretaker. It had been thrust upon her.

As she entered the doorway of the old-fashioned bathroom, the grandfather clock in the hallway chimed the hour. Four o'clock. Almost time to go downstairs and help with dinner.

Ever since Molly had come to live at Rambler's Rest, the house had been open for tours. It wasn't all that profitable during the winter months, but during the vacation season, they did well, since the house was on a tour route that brought in bus loads of people daily. Ever since she had assumed responsibility for

Liz's note four years ago, Molly had started doing dinners for groups of thirty or less. She and Jane, a friend who helped her, usually did four to eight a month, but it was never enough, and it meant extra work, which she didn't look forward to—especially during the school year when she had papers to grade and lessons to prepare.

Tonight they were serving a group of mystery writers who were driving over from New Orleans. She wished she could call the dinner off, crawl back into bed and forget everything—the money, Krystal's problems—all of it. But she couldn't.

As a matter of fact, she needed to get a move on, she thought, dumping lavender bath oil into the water. The group would be arriving in a little over two hours. A faint throb in her temple reminded her that her headache could return at any moment. With a sigh of defeat, she peeled off her clothes and sank into the scented water. It wouldn't be so bad, she thought, sinking up to her chin in bubbles. She would be busy, and the work would take her mind off things. Besides, it was extra money, and every penny counted.

The man slowed the BMW at the driveway, let it crawl the width of the yard and brought it to a stop near the exit. The powerful engine throbbed restlessly. A bus sat in the driveway, and people were milling around outside, which meant she was giving a tour. Masculine lips tightened, drawing on the filter tip of a cigarette. The fire glowed a brighter red, punctuating the dusky darkness for an instant before the man spewed a stream of smoke into the car's plush interior.

He pressed his finger to a button and the window slid down silently. His senses were bombarded with the scent of fresh-cut grass and wild onion, scents he remembered from the childhood he sometimes longed for as an adult, scents that had been replaced by the odors of expensive perfumes, cigarette smoke and money. This pungent country air smelled alive in a way the air of the city never could. He filled his lungs, drawing the familiar odors and their corresponding memories into his very soul. With a sudden sadness he realized he had been farther than just a few states away the last ten years. He had been a lifetime away. And now that he was here, he fully intended to do what he'd set out to do.

His hungry gaze drifted from the lawn, past the bus to the house. It was that peaceful time at day's end— not quite light, but just before the dark gained full control. Lamplight shone through the curtained windows, warding off the darkness, gilding the tops of the shadow-shrouded shrubbery that edged the lower floor . . . luring passersby with the promise of genteel Southern hospitality.

He was grateful that there hadn't been any money to make concessions to modern styles. The house was still white; the shutters were still dark, forest green. In the waning evening light, it looked regal and graceful, just as it always had: like a belle of the South who refused to bow to either the fashion of the day or the insidious ravages of time. Eventually, he thought, it would have to. For as long as the house had been standing, as much history as it had witnessed, those years were still insignificant in the larger scheme of things.

The thought reminded him of his own mortality, and he suddenly understood why Molly O'Connell refused to let go. The restlessness that plagued him so often lately, swept through him, and he jabbed out the cigarette. Understanding what drove her—and himself—didn't change things. Because of her mother's scheming, he had been denied the home that had been in his family for over a century. And, after more than ten years it still chafed. Which was why he'd come back—to do something about it.

The house needed a great deal of work, and the grounds cried out to be put to use. He'd kept in touch with certain people in town; he knew her situation. It was high time Molly O'Connell realized that a face-lift for the house was only postponing the inevitable—like putting a bandage on someone who had just been through major surgery.

He pulled into the driveway behind the bus and turned off the engine. She might as well face the fact that her tenure was over.

It was almost over, Molly thought. The guests were finishing off the evening with coffee and conversation in the two downstairs parlors where her half sister, Cindy, and her friend Jane were available to answer any final questions. It was Molly's chance to steal a breath of fresh air before everyone left and she was faced with the chore of cleaning up.

Stepping out onto the front gallery, she looked out across the yard. A couple of cars sat in the driveway near the bus. She recognized the Toyota as Cindy's; the other was a black BMW. One of Molly's eyebrows lifted in an ironic quirk. Mystery writing must pay well, she thought.

Raising her eyes, she gazed up at the ebony sky. Rain-swollen clouds hid the face of the moon, and the wind whipped her hair across her hot face. An owl hooted. From somewhere across the bayou a mournful *who-who* drifted back. The deep, thrumming bass of bullfrogs mingled with the wild thrashing of Silvie's bells. She hadn't heard the weather report, but there was no doubt they were in for a storm.

A commotion caused her to turn toward the open screen door. The guests were getting ready to leave ... thank goodness. Molly squared her shoulders. It was time to put on her glad-to-have-had-you smile.

By the time the bus pulled out some ten minutes later, she felt as if that same smile were permanently plastered onto her face. Molly kicked off her shoes, picked them up in one hand and padded barefoot across the porch. As she approached the door, she saw a masculine figure on the landing. Had one of the writers been left behind?

His back was to her, and he seemed to be studying the portraits of the Rambler ancestors that graced the wainscotted wall. Molly pulled open the door and stepped inside. The sound sent him spinning on his heel. His inscrutable dark-blue eyes bored down at her.

Her eyes widened, and her breath tangled in her throat. It couldn't be! Her gaze slewed from the man's rough-hewn features to the picture hanging on the wall next to him, a portrait of the first Jonathan Garrett Rambler. With the exception of their clothing, the two men might have been identical twins. The similarities were astounding—from the swath of dark hair that fell across both wide, furrowed foreheads to the grooves that scored their lean shadow-stubbled cheeks. Both had strong, bladelike noses and mouths a woman would die to feel on hers. And, though the portrait was black and white, Molly knew that the ancestor's eyes had been blue, just like the ones staring back at her.

No. There was no mistaking who stood there, no mistaking the joy rising in her heart, despite the fact that he was looking at her as if he would like to tear her limb from limb. And there was no denying that the feelings she thought were dead and buried years ago were gradually stirring to life.

The man standing before her was Jon's son, her stepbrother. The man who had stolen her heart when she was a tender, lovestruck fifteen-year-old.

Jonathan Garrett Rambler the Fifth was back.

Chapter Two

Garrett stared down at her, various emotions storm-
ing the gates of his resentment: guilt that he'd been
caught prowling around the house that was legally
hers, surprise that she'd turned into such a beautiful
woman, and anger that she looked so much like the
stepmother he'd despised.

He was surprised that she looked so mature and had
to remind himself that she was twenty-six. When he
thought of her, as he had done fairly often over the
past ten years, it was as an extremely pretty and
somewhat quiet teenager. She was still extremely
pretty. No. She was more than pretty. Molly O'Connell was gorgeous with her flame-red hair and her skin
as smooth and creamy as gardenia petals.

He hadn't intended to confront her. All he had planned to do was drive out and look things over. Then, when he'd seen the tour group, he'd figured there was no harm in joining them. It had been easy enough to blend in with the other guests as they strolled through the grounds, carrying their mint juleps with them while a teenage girl led the way and answered their questions. He'd been careful to stay well to the back of the crowd while Molly herself gave them the tour of the house.

"Garrett?"

The sound of her voice, hesitant and questioning, broke the silence between them. She was looking up at him, her green eyes filled with disbelief and wariness.

It was amazing how much she looked like Liz, even though her features were softer, more finely drawn. Liz. The thought of her made his blood boil. He fought to suppress the fury he still felt for what she'd done to his father and him. There was no place for anger in his plans, and he hadn't come back to get caught up in bitter memories of the past. He had come to right the wrongs that had been done.

Still, Garrett thought, noticing the way Molly's breasts thrust proudly against the cotton of her blouse, he could see why his father had been taken with Liz. There hadn't been a Rambler born whose head couldn't be turned by a beautiful woman, or a Rambler who wasn't willing to gamble everything he had if something he wanted was at stake. And right now, even though his future was at stake and she counted as an enemy, he wanted Molly O'Connell.

Cursing the Rambler weakness, Garrett's mouth twisted into a mockery of a smile. He started down the stairs, his stylish Italian loafers making hardly a sound on the smooth wood. Stopping in front of her, he plunged his hands into the pockets of his slacks. "Hello, Molly."

He seemed different from the Garrett she had once known.

The thought surprised her, for in her mind, Garrett had always been just . . . Garrett. Eight years her senior, he had been ruggedly handsome, friendly and the source of her daydreams, though he'd had no idea she carried a secret torch for him while he carried a not-so-secret-one for Krystal.

But this stranger with the ice-blue eyes and the implacable jaw wasn't the Garrett who had patiently helped her with her geometry because Liz couldn't spare the time. That Garrett had smiled a great deal and, like Silvie, he'd always been there if she needed someone. That Garrett had taken a little piece of her heart with him when he'd stormed out the door with his father.

"I'll get it back, you scheming bitch. I'll get it back if it's the last thing I do!"

The sudden memory of his parting threat to her mother made her heart race. Why had he come back now, after all this time? Was it possible that he'd heard of her trouble and come back to fulfill his threat?

"Aren't you going to ask me to sit down?"

Molly wondered if the sarcasm she heard in his deep voice was real or a figment of her sudden paranoia. "Of course."

He followed her into the large parlor and sat down on an overstuffed chair, crossing his legs ankle to knee. Molly chose a place in the corner of the Victorian sofa and watched his hungry gaze prowl the room. Without warning, his eyes collided with hers.

"Thirty days, Molly... thirty days..."

Macdonald Henning's ultimatum swept through her troubled mind like the cold, damp breath of winter's winds. She suppressed an involuntary shiver.

No. Garrett's visit wasn't a social one, and he hadn't come back to see her for old times' sake. Intuitively Molly knew that it would be dangerous to give too much of her thoughts and feelings away at this point.

"What brings you back to the swamps?" she asked with all the nonchalance she could muster.

Garrett lifted his arms to the back of the sofa. The gesture pulled the fabric of his shirt across his chest, emphasizing its width. He was an extremely handsome man, she thought with a pang of regret.

"Business," he said, as if the single, succinct word explained everything.

Molly's unease grew. What business? "I hear you live in Atlantic City."

"It's a good place for a gambler."

Her full lips twisted into a wry smile. "Ah, gambling. The Rambler downfall."

Garrett's smile matched hers. "Women are the Rambler downfall."

Molly's gaze shifted from his. He was alluding to Liz's and Jon's divorce and the loss of the plantation. Though it was obvious that the past colored every word of their conversation, she felt it was safer not to comment.

"Actually," he corrected, his voice soft and thick with an unmistakable south Louisiana patois, "this time gambling was the Rambler salvation. But it was hard-going at first."

Twin pangs of embarrassment and guilt for her mother's actions softened Molly's heart and weakened her resolve to be cautious. "I can imagine."

"Can you?" he asked in that soft, sexy voice.

"Yes, I believe I can," she said, mindful of her daily struggle to hang on to Rambler's Rest.

For some reason, he chose not to pursue her last statement. His steady gaze quickened her heartbeats. "How's your dad?" he asked, instead.

"He's fine."

"And Krystal?"

The fact that he'd asked about Krystal threw Molly for a moment. The hurt she'd felt at fifteen, knowing that Garrett was interested in Krys, resurfaced, though it was muted by the passage of time. Was it possible that he still felt something for her sister?

"She's fine," Molly told him. "She and her husband are spending some time in Greece. How're Shiloh and Jon?" she countered. She didn't want to talk about her sister.

"Shiloh is breaking hearts all along the East coast, and Dad's great," Garrett said. "He remarried Shiloh's mother again three years ago. Ellen's a wonderful woman, and they're very happy.''

There it was again. The less-than-subtle reference to their mutual past. He didn't say it, but the implication was clear: Jon's Ellen was everything Molly's own mother hadn't been. Molly's heart began to throb painfully, like the ache in a sore tooth.

"I'm glad," she said with sincerity. "I always cared a lot for Jon. He deserves to be happy."

"I'll tell him you said so."

Civilized. That's what their conversation was. Civilized. Garrett was polite, but not friendly. There were enough undercurrents in the room to light the entire house, yet they were dancing around whatever issue was at stake...whatever it was that he had come back for.

His gaze raked the room's contents once again. "I see you still have the Landseer." He cut his eyes back to hers, startling her.

"Of course I have the Landseer. Surely you know that I'd never get desperate enough to sell the paintings," she told him, her chin lifting a fraction. "I'd sell myself first."

His dark eyebrows quirked in question. "Are things desperate, then *Petite*?"

His voice was soft, his tone coaxing, and Molly couldn't help the way her heartbeats stumbled at his unexpected use of her pet name. For a moment, she was tempted to unburden her heart. Maybe he hadn't changed so much after all. Maybe the uncomfortable feelings between them were nothing but the inevitable changes affecting people as they matured.

Her eyes met the gemstone hardness of his, and she knew she was fooling herself.

He blames me!

The realization screamed through Molly's brain, brilliant in its clarity. Garrett's actions and attitude suddenly became clear. She didn't know why he had come back to Louisiana, but his arrival had brought him face-to-face with the bitter pain of the past. Had the passage of time made him forget that his father had been unfaithful to her mother? Though Liz's retaliation had been extreme, she'd had just reason to seek a divorce.

"I'm sorry," she told him, knowing the words were inadequate. "I know what happened back then was painful for you and Jon. But what he did was wrong."

A slight blush crept up over Garrett's whisker-stubbled cheeks. He pushed himself from the chair and crossed to the window, his tanned hand kneading the back of his neck. Suddenly, he pivoted to face her. "I haven't forgotten, and I haven't forgotten what your mother said the day the divorce became final, either."

Molly's forehead puckered in a frown. She'd been gone that day, visiting a friend in Houma. All she remembered was a sense of desolation when her mother told her and Krystal that she was divorcing Jon.

"Liz told my father that she'd only married him because he was a 'stepping stone.' She said that she'd always known he wouldn't be able to stay away from other women, but that it didn't really matter, because if she waited long enough he'd get careless and she'd get everything she wanted.''

He laughed, a caustic sound that echoed off the walls of the parlor. "She planned to take him to the cleaners from the minute she found out about Rambler's Rest. Even Krystal knew it. She thought the whole thing was funny.''

Molly couldn't hide her shock. She'd known her mother was socially ambitious and a bit of a schemer, but she'd never dreamed that she would sink to such depths. If Garrett was telling the truth, what Liz had done to Jon bordered on the criminal. No wonder Garrett was so bitter. And—right or wrong—it was becoming clear that much of the resentment Garrett felt toward her mother had tainted whatever feelings he'd once had for her. A sense of loss brought an ache to her heart.

"I didn't know," she said, her voice hardly above a whisper. "I...I don't know what to say. I certainly can't make excuses for my mother. She was just...Liz. She and Krystal have always been different. I've loved them both, but I've never understood them.''

"Love!" Garrett spat. "How can you possibly love anyone as selfish as those two?''

Molly felt as if he'd struck her. Her chin lifted, and her voice hardened. "The same way you can love a two-timer, I suppose.''

"It isn't the same! Liz was nothing but a liar and a cheat.''

His accusation hurt, more than Molly thought possible. Trembling, filled with confused emotions, she stood up. "I'm not going to trade insults with you, Garrett. It's one skill my mother never taught me. What happened in the past was between our parents and doesn't concern us." She started for the door. "I think you'd better leave."

"Not so fast." His hand closed around her upper arm, and he hauled her around to face him.

Molly gasped. She hadn't even heard him move. Outside, rumbling thunder issued a warning. A gust of refreshing wind blew the scent of rain-washed earth through the open door, and the bells of the wind chimes thrashed wildly in the night. Her wide-eyed gaze climbed from the hand gripping her bare flesh to his hard, unyielding features. He was so close she could see the tiny lines at the corners of his eyes and the shattered-glass pattern of darker blue in his irises.

"Doesn't concern us?" he said in a voice so quiet that it frightened her more than outright fury. "You're living in the house that has been in my family for more than a hundred and thirty years, a house I grew up in and which should rightfully be mine some day—and it doesn't concern us?"

Molly didn't want to think about that. She couldn't. Not when he was so close. She drew in a ragged breath. The smell of his cologne, musky and masculine, filled her nostrils. His hand was warm and his body so close she could feel the pressure of his thighs against hers. Her tongue slicked out over lips gone as dry as the Sahara, leaving a sheen of moisture that clung to the curved surface of her mouth.

Garrett followed the movement of her tongue with eyes that had turned a hazy gray. She felt the sudden tenseness in him and heard the harsh inhalation of his breath. Her fear and anger vanished along with whatever bit of sanity she possessed, overcome by her rising awareness of him. She thought she saw his head tilt toward hers as it had so many times in the past . . . in her dreams.

"Molly!"

The sound of Jane Avery's voice preceded her into the room and broke the spell of madness binding them. Garrett released his hold on Molly, spinning away so quickly that she stumbled and had to grab the back of a damask-covered Queen Anne chair for support.

"Do you want me to..." Jane's speech trailed away when she saw Garrett. "Excuse me," she said glancing from him to Molly. "I didn't know you had company."

"I was just leaving." Garrett started across the worn Aubusson carpet toward the door.

Without a word, Molly turned and watched him go, wrapping her arms tightly around her upper body to ward off a chill that had nothing to do with the damp air permeating the room.

When he reached the door he turned, his eyes raking her from head to toe. "I'll see you later."

He disappeared into the violent, windswept night before she could think of a suitable reply. To Molly, the words sounded like both a promise and a threat.

Garrett strode out of the house and down the wooden steps, his heart beating an angry cadence with his footfalls. Raindrops, whipped about by the gusting wind, peppered him. A bolt of lightning seared the sky, and the answering thunder rolled like cannonballs across the heavens.

He broke into a sprint and reached the BMW seconds before the leaden skies opened. Without pausing, he turned the key and the engine purred to life. He pulled through the circular driveway, spraying white shells behind him.

Dammit!

He'd saved and plotted and worked for this moment for years, and now, when it was within his grasp, he'd almost let his anger sabotage everything. He, of all people, knew the importance of playing his cards right. It had all seemed so simple when he'd thought it through. Thanks to Macdonald Henning at the bank, who was still a good friend of Jon's, Garrett was aware of Molly's financial situation. She was about to lose the place. He wanted it back. He'd offered her a more-than-fair price—enough that she could make a new start.

He didn't know why he wanted to do it that way, except that he had known from the first day Jon had brought her to the plantation that Molly loved the place as much as he did. She belonged there, and he knew how devastating leaving would be. Besides, he'd always liked her as a kid. She was different from her mother and sister. Quieter. Even a little insecure. Like any teenager, she'd needed the support of a caring mother, but Liz had been too busy doing whatever it was that grasping, scheming women did, and Molly had been left to her own devices, except for the times she spent with her father. Hell, he supposed he was getting soft and sentimental the older he got.

A savage gust of wind rocked the car, reminding Garrett to keep his mind on his driving. He gripped the steering wheel tighter and tried to figure out what had thrown him off stride. Seeing the house in the dusk had kindled a deep sorrow for all the years he'd been deprived of his legacy. Tagging along during the tour had been a mistake, an impulse he'd soon regretted. As he'd listened to Molly and the young girl recount the plantation's colorful history, his sorrow had grown . . . along with resentment and anger.

He'd never thought he would see Molly face-to-face, and that's when it had all begun to fall apart.

He'd known how risky it was to sneak upstairs while the meal was being served, but after looking the grounds over, he'd needed to see the house for himself . . . alone. It hadn't taken him long to know he'd made a mistake. He wasn't prepared for the barrage of memories—memories of past Christmases, his friends coming over after ball games, horseback riding through the adjacent woods. Those memories had overwhelmed him, and he'd lost track of time.

The sound of the bus leaving had startled him, and he was about to sneak downstairs and out the back door before anyone was the wiser. If he hadn't stopped to look at Nate Rambler's portrait, he might have succeeded. Instead, Molly had caught him snooping around.

When he'd turned to see her standing near the front door, looking so much like her gorgeous mother, his remorse had changed quickly and frighteningly to fury, no matter how misplaced he knew it was.

She wasn't the Molly he remembered. She wasn't shy and quiet anymore. There was fire in her eyes and a challenge in her voice, two traits no red-blooded Rambler male could claim immunity to. That he'd responded to her nearness on a purely sexual level was more unsettling than he cared to admit. If her friend Jane hadn't come in, he knew he would have kissed her. And even more disturbing than that, he knew she would have let him. He couldn't afford getting involved with anyone—especially not with her.

Garrett pulled into the hotel parking lot, turned off the ignition and closed his eyes. He'd sworn he was through with women except for the most basic of needs, but that didn't jibe with the pull of Molly's soft, green gaze. His curse matched the fury of the storm. Hadn't Jon's failed relationships taught him anything? Hadn't he learned anything about scheming and lying women from his brief encounter with Krystal? And hadn't his own flash-in-the-pan marriage to Lacey shown him that vows meant nothing to a woman, that love was just a word?

Molly might be different from her mother and sister, but she was still a woman. And no woman could be that different.

Forget it, Rambler! Dredging up the past isn't going to change things. And whether you like it or not, Molly O'Connell turns you on.

He scraped his hand down his whiskered face. All he had to do was keep his mind on his reasons for coming back.

Rambler's Rest. His past. And, if he had his way, his future. He couldn't believe it when Mac Henning had told him Molly had turned down his offer. It meant he'd have to wait the thirty days and go through all that legal brouhaha before he could take possession.

Possession. How long could she hang on? Could she possibly make the thirty day ultimatum the bank had given her? Mac Henning said it was amazing how she continued to find the money when her back was to the wall. How did she do it? Did she rely on a man—or men—the way her mother had?

"I'd sell myself first."

The possibility that she had turned out like her mother left a bad taste in his mouth, but it was a possibility he had to consider.

The hotel room was carefully appointed and seductively lit. The sound of a key turning in the lock made the dark-haired woman propped up in the middle of the bed look up from the magazine she was reading.

A tall, well-built, expensively dressed man stepped through the door.

The woman laid her magazine aside. "How did it go?"

"Well enough. I found out a couple of things of importance."

"Oh?"

"First of all, the paintings are still there. I'm not sure about the jewelry. Furthermore, he's broke. He couldn't buy a bag of peanuts at the circus."

She rubbed the tip of one burgundy-polished nail over the fullness of her bottom lip as she tried to put together all the pieces. "So the money is—"

"—a front to land him rich women, whom he milks for all they're worth before discarding them and going on to new prey. No offense, darling," he said, sitting down on the bed, "but he thought that acquiring the plantation would be quite a coup. Then he found out it was mortgaged to the hilt and that there wasn't much left to sell off, except the jewelry and a couple of paintings. Obviously, he still thought it was worth a go." His mouth curled into a grin. "Enough so that he dumped you."

Her mouth twisted at the memory, but she held her temper. The past was past, and she had bigger fish to fry. "How interesting. Then I guess it's worth a go for us, too."

Between the incessant rumblings of the storm and the memory of Garrett's unexpected visit, Molly hardly slept at all. She stared up at the ceiling while her mind replayed their argument—recapturing every nuance, every innuendo. As she had the night before, she wondered what had brought him back and prayed that his reasons had nothing to do with her current predicament.

By dawn, just as the storm ended and the sun began its ascent, she was no closer to an answer than she had been when she'd fallen wearily into bed. Some things, however, were very clear, and she didn't like the deductions she'd made. She flopped onto her back. The damp sheets twisted around her slender hips and she threw her forearm over her gritty eyes to block out the mocking brightness of the early morning sunshine.

Garrett Rambler was obviously still scarred by the things that had happened between their parents. That saddened her, as did the knowledge that the way he felt about her so long ago had changed. Her disappointment was silly, especially since she never expected to see him again. Still, whenever she thought about him, it was with the gentleness that accompanies the fond recollections of young love.

Sadness drew a deep sigh from her. She remembered how she'd spun fanciful, romantic daydreams about being married to Garrett. Reality had proven that marriage was far from the stuff that dreams were made of, but something inside her clung to a hope that maybe there were such things as true romantic love and happy marriages.

Her inability to find anything that remotely resembled true love had kept her from saying yes to the half-dozen proposals she'd received through the years. Besides, she'd never been able to picture another man in the house....

The sudden sound of dripping water caught her attention and sent her heart plummeting to her toes. *No, please,* she thought as she lowered her feet to the stool sitting beside the high bed. *Don't let the roof be leaking.*

But her prayers were futile. In the wide upper hall, water dripped onto the floor with a steady rhythm, and the drip was rapidly becoming a stream. The roof had leaked, and the water had pooled in a low place in the ceiling. The *bousillage*—a mixture of animal hair, mud and Spanish moss—which had been used to plaster the ceilings and walls, was already starting to loosen and fall.

Like a child she wanted to lie down on the floor and kick and scream and rail against the Fates. Didn't she have enough problems without this? Angrily, she dashed away the tears with her fingertips. There was no telling how extensive the damage was...or how much money it would take to fix it.

It was worse than she expected. Wooden shingles were scattered across the roof and lawn. The rain had left several large water spots on the ceilings of the second floor, and a branch had blown from a tree on the far side of the house, shattering several panes of a bedroom window. The fact that the almost-impossible-to-replace feather mattress was ruined was the least of her problems.

She went to the kitchen and poured herself a cup of strong chicory-laced coffee; then she began phoning repairmen and a local expert on mending the *bousillage*. Thirty minutes later, she buried her face in her hands and bowed to defeat.

It was bad enough having to come up with the back payments on the house. Now she was faced with the extra expense of rain damage repairs. Past experience told her the costs would significantly eat into what money she had, putting her even more in the red. And, like the bank, the repairs wouldn't wait.

She wiped a weary, errant tear with the hem of her nightshirt and reached for the receiver again. The only thing left to do was to call Macdonald Henning and tell him she'd decided to accept the offer to sell, after all. She punched in the bank's telephone number and waited to be put through to his private office.

Less than five minutes later, the appointment made for that very afternoon, Molly hung up the phone and gave way to the scalding flow of tears held in check for too long. She'd done all she could. She had no choice. No other house would ever be home to her, but she supposed she would survive.

Jon and Garrett had.

At five minutes before two o'clock, Molly stepped resolutely into the cool air-conditioned bank and walked toward Mac Henning's office. She wore a peach, scoop-necked, sleeveless linen sheath with large white buttons marching down the front closure. Oversize earrings, heels and a straw bag, all in pure white, completed her ensemble, which she hoped made her look cool, cheerful and collected.

In fact, she was miserable. It had taken her a full hour to cover the ravages left by her tears, and, even after cold cloths and generous dollops of eye drops her eyes looked puffy and watery... as if she'd cried long and hard, which, of course, she had. Even now, it was a struggle to keep the tears back.

She knocked on Mac Henning's door, and he called out a booming "Come in." Drawing a steadying breath and simulating a pleasant smile, Molly turned the doorknob and stepped inside.

Mac rose from behind his massive mahogany desk, rounding it with his hand outstretched. "Good to see you again, my dear. My, don't you look pretty?"

"Thank you," Molly said as his soft, pampered hand swallowed hers in a flaccid handshake.

As the banker released his hold, a movement in her peripheral vision snagged Molly's attention. She turned, and her eyes widened in surprise. Garrett stood near the window, his hands, as usual, resting in his pockets. There was nothing menacing about either his actions or the look on his face; nonetheless, a terrible suspicion began to grow, leeching the last bit of color from her pale cheeks.

"What are you doing here?" she whispered through stiff lips.

The question was redundant. She knew what he was doing there.

Garrett was back after ten years. On business. And he had plenty of money. She'd wondered why he'd come by the night before, and now his reason was clear. He was checking out his future investment. Garrett Rambler was Mac Henning's buyer for Rambler's Rest.

Chapter Three

Molly didn't think; she reacted. Without a word, she turned and started toward the door.

"Molly? What is it?"

She didn't acknowledge Mac Henning's concerned query. The polished brass doorknob was in her hand when she felt Garrett's grip on her arm, in a repeat performance of his gesture the night before.

He jerked her around to face him, pulling her so close they were almost nose to nose. This time, no physical awareness pulsated between them. There was only the accumulation of years of anger. Garrett's blue eyes were ice cold as his gaze penetrated hers. "Where do you think you're going?"

"Anywhere away from you. I don't do business

with sneaks," she said, enunciating each word carefully. Across the room, Mac Henning gasped.

"Sneaks! What are you talking about?"

"Sneaks," she reiterated, her eyes flashing with green fire. "If you aren't sneaking around, explain why Mac didn't tell me yesterday you were the buyer. And why did you come to the house last night and *sneak* upstairs? So you could check the place out—right? So you could make sure you weren't getting a pig in a poke!" She pulled her arm free. "Well, Garrett, how did it measure up? Have I taken care of the place to your satisfaction?"

Again Garrett shoved his hands into his pockets. "As a matter of fact," he snapped, "you haven't. The land is just lying there. It should be put to use."

Molly couldn't believe what she was hearing. A bitter laugh escaped her lips. "Well, pardon me for not going out and putting in a whole new industry, but I've had my hands full trying to keep the roof over my head."

She looked at Mac, who had returned to his chair and was regarding the exchange with a mixture of disbelief and morbid fascination. "I'm sorry, Mr. Henning. The deal's off—unless you can find another buyer."

He nodded, too shocked to speak.

"You can't walk out of here," Garrett said.

Filled with defiance, her eyes met his. "Just watch me." Without another word, Molly turned and stalked out of the office, only partly aware of the curious looks she was getting from the people in the lobby.

Riding the crest of her anger, she pushed through the door and started down the steps. The humid air was like a slap in the face after the coolness of the bank's interior. She was halfway to her car when she heard Garrett call her name. She ignored him, reached her battered Escort and concentrated on unlocking the door.

Escape was imminent when Garrett grabbed her again. He turned her around to face him, imprisoning her between the car and his body. Her angry gaze met his.

"Did anyone ever tell you your manners are less than charming?" she asked, her lips curled with sarcasm. "You're gonna do that to someone someday and get the surprise of your life."

Something in her eyes caused him to release her and take a step backward. "It might not be necessary if you'd stop running away and would agree to carry on a conversation like an adult."

"I don't have anything to say to you, and I think I heard enough of what you had to say last night." She got into the car and shut the door.

With a few sharp words, Garrett told her what she could do with last night. Resting his forearm on top of the car, he leaned toward the open window. "Why are you being so stubborn? It's a relatively uncomplicated situation."

In response, Molly cranked the engine and shoved the gearshift into reverse, forcing him to walk beside the Ford as she backed out.

"Stop the car, dammit!"

Instead she put the car into drive and pressed the accelerator. In frustration, Garrett hit the rear fender with his hand as she sped toward the street.

As she pulled away, Molly glanced into her rearview mirror. Garrett stood in the middle of the parking lot watching her drive away, his hands on his hips and a look of disgust on his handsome face.

Her heart lurched in pain. For a moment, she was tempted to turn around and go back, but pride, the intangible curse that kept her from asking for help, wouldn't let her.

In her mind, she retraced her steps into the bank and rekindled the feeling of betrayal when she'd realized Garrett was the buyer. Anger surfaced once more, erasing the ache in her heart. Darn Garrett, anyway! Did he think that because he had money he could just come back and *buy* her home out from under her? And did the fact that he could do so make it right?

The Garrett she'd known years ago would have known how much she was hurting. And he wouldn't have rubbed salt into the wound.

The day after his explosive encounter with Molly, Garrett was holed up in his motel room, contemplating his next move. He reckoned he should go back to Atlantic City and let time and the legal system take care of matters, but for some reason, he couldn't bring himself to leave. Instead, he paced and cursed Molly O'Connell's stubbornness. And her beauty.

It was twenty-four hours after the confrontation at the bank, and he was still battling his reaction to the way the linen sheath she had worn accentuated the creaminess of her complexion and the swell of her breasts. He'd obviously been without a woman too long. Otherwise, Molly O'Connell would be the last one he'd choose.

Forget her, Rambler.

Right. He would. Just as soon as he put a few states between them. Which brought him back to his present dilemma. Why did Molly want to make this so hard on them both by refusing to face the truth? Why couldn't she see the advantages of his buying the plantation instead of fighting him at every turn? After all, what was more natural than for Rambler's Rest to revert to the original owners? She either sold the place to him or she lost it, at which time he would buy it anyway. The only difference was that if she accepted his offer now, she would come out with some money of her own.

A memory he'd been shying away from slipped through his mind: Molly's face as she'd led the tour through the house on the day he first stopped by. Though she was tired, there was no mistaking the pride and pleasure in her eyes as she recounted the tale of the first Jonathan Garrett Rambler and his bride, Lisette. It occurred to him with something of a shock that Molly's losing the plantation would be more than hard on her. It would be devastating ... just as it had been for him.

Still, the old idealistic Molly would have seen his side. She would have wanted the house to belong to someone who loved it as much as she did. Garrett ran an agitated hand through his dark hair. Maybe he'd give it one more shot. He'd drive out to Rambler's Rest and try to reason with her one last time.

He ignored his heart's whispering that said he just wanted to see her.

It was midafternoon when Garrett pulled into the driveway. Another tour bus was parked in front of the house. He got out of his car and saw that Cindy, Molly's pretty teenage half sister, had a small group touring the grounds and antique shop. Molly was probably taking the others through the house. He pocketed his keys and strode up the wide front steps. Without knocking, he entered the double screen doors. More than twenty-five adults crowded around Molly in the spacious hallway, while she explained how the support of the hanging stairway worked.

The sound of the screen door closing brought her gaze to his. She was surprised to see him, but defiance quickly replaced the emotion. Garrett couldn't help the half smile that tugged at his lips. There wasn't much she could do or say with so many people around.

To his surprise, she smiled, too. But before he recognized the taunting tilt of her lips, she made a sweeping gesture in his direction. "You're in luck today," she told the group.

Every head turned toward him, and Garrett was momentarily disconcerted.

"This is Mr. Garrett Rambler," Molly continued, "one of the direct descendants of Nathan Rambler.

I'm certain he'll be glad to take you upstairs and show you the *bousillage* and the balcony where Silvia Antilly fell to her death, while I go and fix us some refreshments.''

"Isn't she the ghost who is supposed to haunt the house?" a young woman asked Garrett.

A titter of skeptical laughter swept the crowd, and Molly took the opportunity to slip from the room. Garrett watched her go and wondered if she'd hoped to throw him off guard by suggesting that he take over the tour. If so, she was in for a disappointment. He'd been doing tours longer than she'd lived in the house.

"Yes, it's true. She is supposed to haunt this house," he supplied easily.

"Have you ever seen the ghost, Mr. Rambler?"

Garrett's gaze shifted from the slight sway of Molly's hips to the attractive woman. He smiled. "I've never seen her," he said truthfully, "but I've heard her laughing."

Uneasy laughter rippled through the room.

He smiled again. His confession seldom failed to convert a few disbelievers. He supposed it was because he didn't look like the type to make up ghost stories. "Silvie isn't a bad ghost, though she does love a good prank. One of her favorite tricks is to come in while you're sleeping at night, take all the covers off the bed and pile them in the corner."

"Aw, come on!" came a masculine voice from the middle of the crowd. "Gimme a break!"

Garrett shrugged good-naturedly and started for the stairs. "Enough talk of ghosts. If you'll follow me, we'll go upstairs, and I'll show you a rolling pin made especially for smoothing out a feather bed.''

Garrett stood beside Molly on the wide gallery and watched the bus pull away. For the last hour or so, the unspoken truce between them had brought back memories and weakened his resolve. He didn't want to fight with her.

"Tired?"

Her wary gaze flew to his. She nodded. "A little."

Ducking her head, she brushed past him and went into the house. He followed, and, just as he reached to take her arm in what was becoming a habitual gesture, she turned. Guiltily, he rammed his hands into his pockets.

"Stop running away from it, Molly," he said, his voice rough with embarrassment. "You're gonna have to face it sooner or later."

Molly raised her chin. "I'd rather do it later, I suppose. Losing this place..." Her voice, husky with emotion, trailed away. She reached down to pick up two empty glasses and looked back at him.

"Do you know that until I came to live here, we'd never lived in one place much longer than a year? Rambler's Rest is the only real home I've ever had." She looked around the room, a wistful smile on her lips. "I can still remember the first time I saw the house. Jon had just told me a little about Nate, Lisette and Silvie, and, since I was always a history buff anyway, I was hooked."

Garrett wasn't sure he wanted to hear any more, but he seemed to have no choice as Molly continued.

"Then he pulled into the driveway, and there was the house. I couldn't believe it. Rambler's Rest wasn't as pretty or as grand as some of the other houses, but it looked sturdy and permanent...as if it would be the same forever. I think I fell in love with the house right then. And the house loved me back." She shrugged and shook her head, at the absurdity of what she was saying. "Crazy, huh?"

Garrett recalled how he'd been thinking earlier that she'd belonged there from the very first. Without being aware of it, his manner softened. "Not so crazy. As Aunt Lisbet would have said, the house accepted your presence."

Molly was hardly aware that she was telling her innermost feelings to the man who was trying to oust her from the house she loved. For the moment, he was just Garrett...the Garrett she remembered. "I wouldn't say that too loudly," she cautioned. "Someone might think you're ready for Pineville."

Her laughter was soft and throaty. And incredibly sexy.

"It isn't crazy, and neither was Aunt Lisbet." He paused. "Well, not *too* crazy," he amended, eliciting another laugh from Molly. "Aunt Lisbet always said houses had personalities. They were happy or sad because of the things that happened in them."

"And what is Rambler's Rest?"

"It's a happy house, even though Silvie and Henri died here. She said that all the happiness that came afterward negated their deaths. She always thought that because it's the young, mischievous Silvie's ghost who haunts the place it means she's trying to bring back the joy the house deserves before she finds her own rest.''

One of Molly's eyebrows lifted. ''That's pretty weird, Garrett. Why haven't I ever heard about this before?''

There was a hint of humor in her eyes, and his lips curved in a slight smile—the first she'd seen since he'd come back. ''We don't talk about Aunt Lisbet's theories much, if you know what I mean.''

Molly's heartbeats stumbled at the sight of such masculine beauty. Why did her nemesis have to be so devilishly handsome?

''Think about your mother and Krystal. Their lives here were filled with a series of accidents.''

He had a point. Molly could think of several mishaps without even trying. A sprained ankle, a ruptured appendix, a broken toe, a second-degree burn... Her eyes met his. ''Coincidences.''

''Were they?'' His gaze held hers.

She drew in a deep breath, bent to pick up the tray and started for the kitchen. This was a bit much, even for someone as suggestible as she was.

Garrett watched the way the fabric of her skirt pulled across her hips and felt his blood begin to race in true Rambler fashion. Why did she have to grow up to be such a heartbreaker? Why couldn't she have been homely? It would have made his job much easier. As it was, his growing desire for her kept interfering with his desire to reclaim his birthright. Hadn't the past taught him anything? He reminded himself of his reason for coming back. A hard edge crept into his voice.

"Do us both a favor."

Molly turned, surprised to hear the hardness back in his voice, after they'd just spent the better part of an hour together without arguing. "What?"

A few long strides took him to within a foot of her. "Sell me the plantation. My offer is more than generous."

"I can't," she said with a shake of her head.

Garrett swore in exasperation and took her shoulders with the intention of shaking some sense into her, but the elusive scent of her perfume and the feel of her soft flesh beneath his hands swamped his senses. He didn't want to shake her; he wanted to kiss her until she couldn't say no anymore...to anything.

The knowledge that she had her own particular brand of power fueled his irritation. "Give it up, Molly," he said. "It would take a miracle for you to come up with the money in time."

Her eyes widened by degrees, as if she were witnessing some horrible scene in her mind. She moved away from his grasp. "I can't give up. I'll get the money somehow."

"How?" he snapped. "We both know that miracles don't happen anymore."

"I don't know," she said. "I'll think of something."

*   *   *

When Molly returned from the kitchen, Garrett was gone. A feeling of loss, that had nothing to do with losing the house, lasted throughout her solitary meal and the remainder of the evening.

After the ten o'clock news, she went to bed, but not to sleep. That comfort was denied her troubled mind. Instead, she watched the moonshadows dance across her curtained bedroom and let her mind journey back to the times she and Garrett had shared when she'd first come to Rambler's Rest. She remembered how she'd guarded her secret school-girl crush and how she'd fought her jealousy over his attraction to Krystal. And, she would never forget the day Krystal had told her that Garrett was seeing not only her but her best friend, as well.

Molly threw one arm over her face, hiding her aching, tear-filled eyes from the moon-drenched night. Too bad she'd been too naive and innocent to see his true colors. She'd loved Garrett Rambler back then. Loved him with the purity and fervor of her fifteen-year-old heart. And why not? With his broad shoulders, wavy black hair and incredible blue eyes, he was a young girl's dream.

He'd changed. No doubt about that. He was harder than she imagined a man could be. And he was angry. But Garrett Rambler was still a dream, as her body reminded her every time he touched her. Maturity had broadened his physique even more. He looked fit and healthy, despite the dissolute life-style she supposed went with running a gambling casino.

He wanted her. She could feel the desire arcing between them every time he touched her. She'd seen it in his eyes before Jane interrupted them the night he'd first come back, the night he'd almost kissed her.

She drew in a trembling breath. She wished the house weren't an issue between them. She wished she had a chance to get to know him as an adult, a chance to explore the undeniable attraction between them without strife or disagreements to separate them. The longing for someone to love her—a longing Molly thought she'd buried inside her—filled her to the bursting point, even though she knew it was ridiculous to feel that longing for Garrett Rambler.

Driven by indecision and restlessness, she climbed down from the high bed and crossed the room to stand by the open window. The bayou wound through the landscape like a silvery ribbon through ebony hair. If she left, would she ever see all this again?

Forget the past, Molly. Think about your future.

The mild reprimand ended the depressing turn of her thoughts. She focused instead on how Garrett would manage to run his casino and the plantation at the same time . . . when he took it over, as she knew he eventually would.

There! She'd done it! She'd acknowledged her worst fear. As Garrett said, she couldn't run away from the situation forever. She might as well face facts. Coming up with the money *would* take a miracle, and miracles were in short supply these days.

"I can't get the money, Silvie," she said aloud, admitting defeat for the first time. "So the bank will take over the house, and Garrett will buy it. I guess I should take Mac Henning's suggestion and sell. I'd at least make a little profit.''

She sighed. The problem was, she didn't want profit. She wanted to stay at Rambler's Rest, yet she had no idea how she could bring that dream to reality. Molly chewed her bottom lip. Why the heck did Garrett want the place if he was going to be in New Jersey? she wondered. He couldn't be in two places at once. A nebulous, farfetched idea tiptoed through her mind. It made sense that if his casino was successful, he would need someone to take care of the house in his absence. Maybe, she thought with a growing hope, he would hire her as a housekeeper...a caretaker to see that things went smoothly while he was gone.

The ingeniousness of her idea made Molly smile into the moonlit darkness. She would play on his logic and business acumen. If necessary, she would resort to playing on his sympathy. Surely the friendship they shared in the past would stand her in good stead for a job—even if he had despised her mother.

By dawn, Molly had her speech to Garrett rehearsed. The plan, however, did have pitfalls. She would have to be on guard whenever he was around. He was too handsome, too worldly. And if she wasn't careful, he would steal her heart all over again...if he hadn't already.

Sleeplessness drove Garrett from his bed in the early morning hours; restlessness drove him to his car, and something he couldn't explain drove him to the Bayou

Lafourche. Parking where he could see the house, he got out of the car and rested his forearms across the top.

A full moon still hung in the sky, its brilliance turning the sluggish waters to molten silver. It was hard to imagine the bayou as a major shipping thoroughfare, almost impossible to picture barges and riverboats navigating its twists and turns. Thinking of the plantation's colorful history brought a lump to his throat. Most people would consider a grown man who got emotional about a house and a piece of land a real jerk. But few people ever had the chance to own a slice of history. *I'll get the money somehow. I'll think of something.* Molly's words, spoken last night, haunted him.

Staring at the house, he reached for a cigarette. Was she asleep, dreaming whatever dreams single women dreamed, or was she awake, thinking over her options? Even as he asked himself the question, he thought he saw movement at her bedroom window. He imagined he could see her standing there, looking at the night, wondering what she would do when she left Rambler's Rest.

"I'll get the money somehow. I'll think of something. I'd sell myself first." The words, whispered on the soft, humid wind flowing along the bayou, played through his mind. He pictured Molly on a auction block, prepared to go to the highest bidder, and grinned wryly. He was getting fanciful. And tired.

But he didn't leave, and his thoughts refused to give him any rest. He remembered the way his body responded every time he got near her. Molly O'Connell made him feel things he'd rather not feel for any woman...especially not for her, but he knew there was no sense lying to himself. He wanted her. Badly.

Molly rose at dawn and started to make coffee. She was fixing a bowl of cereal when she heard a knock at the back door. Tightening the belt of her short robe and wondering who on earth would be calling at six o'clock in the morning, she went to answer it.

When she pulled open the kitchen door, she saw Garrett standing there. "What are you doing here?" she asked, marginally aware that he needed a shave.

The grim lines bracketing his mouth tightened. He shrugged. "I've been up all night."

Molly hoped her surprise didn't show. What was bothering Garrett so much he couldn't sleep? "Come in," she said, stepping aside.

Garrett complied, settling himself at the table while Molly busied herself with getting cups from the cabinet. Mugs in hand, she turned to face him. "Garrett..." She paused, uncertain, now that he was standing before her in the clear light of day, if the idea spawned by the night and her desperation was a good one.

"What?" he asked with a frown.

She turned to pour coffee, took a deep breath and plunged in. "I started thinking last night that if you go back to New Jersey to run your casino, you'll need someone to stay here and take care of things."

He didn't say anything. Molly turned with the full mugs. There was a look in his eyes, as if he knew what she was going to say next.

"No," he said, instinctively knowing what she was proposing and more angry than he would have believed possible. "I'm not going to hire you to take care of the house for me."

"Why not?" she cried, setting the mugs down with double *thuds*. "You could go away and not have to worry about a thing."

"Forget it."

The last of her hopes evaporated. Anger at the unfairness of life rose like a tide inside her. Desperation added fierceness to her voice. "I won't forget it! Hire me, Garrett," she stormed. "I want to stay here. I'll do anything you want. I'll be your cook, your housekeeper . . . anything."

I'll get the money somehow. I'd sell myself . . .

Garrett's heated gaze moved over her scantily clad body. Her defiance died, and awareness replaced it. She could see the hunger in his eyes.

"Anything?"

She swallowed hard, and her chin climbed a degree higher. "Anything," she said, her voice nothing but a wisp of sound.

Garrett couldn't believe what he was hearing. He shook his head. "You'd do that? Sleep with me, become my mistress, just to stay in this house?"

Molly wrapped her arms around her upper body and nodded.

He considered the look of determination on her face for a moment. "Sorry," he told her unsmilingly. "I don't want a mistress."

Molly's bravado crumbled as shame coursed through her. She turned away and gripped the countertop. Dear God, she'd promised to give this man her body without the sanctity of marriage, and he'd turned her down.

She heard him scoot his chair out. Good. He was leaving her alone with her misery and embarrassment. But instead of hearing the door open and close she heard him say, "I won't take you for my mistress, Molly, but I will take you for my wife."

Chapter Four

Molly whirled around. Garrett was standing at the back door, looking out at the garden as if he'd asked her what kind of roses she grew instead of just having proposed marriage. Her heart thundered, and she had to lean against the cabinets for support.

"Wife?" she parroted in a voice saturated in disbelief.

He turned and surveyed her from her bare feet to the top of her fiery-haired head. His gaze lingered a bit longer than necessary on the thrust of her breasts beneath the soft cotton nightshirt, then ambled to her mouth. "Why not? It isn't a bad idea, and it'll solve both our problems."

Molly felt a rush of heat. His meaning was obvious. He wanted her. If they married, he'd get her, and she'd get to stay. But wasn't that the same setup they'd have if she was his mistress? It didn't make sense, and somehow marriage seemed so...real. So final. She supposed that somewhere in her subconscious, she'd clung to the knowledge that if she was his mistress, she could leave if and when she wanted.

While the reality of life had shown her that marriage was a far cry from the romantic scenarios on television and in books and certainly didn't always last forever, a part of her refused to abandon the idealistic image of "happily ever after." But Garrett's cold-blooded proposal to solve both their problems—as he put it—was the most preposterous suggestion anyone had ever made to her.

Garrett said marriage wasn't a bad idea, and he was right. It was madness. And to accept would be pure stupidity. Marriage wouldn't solve their problems; it would create new ones.

"I can't marry you," she said, shaking her head and refusing to let her eyes meet his.

Garrett crossed the room and took her chin between his thumb and fingers, lifting her head until their eyes met. His expression was as hard as the hand holding her chin.

"Why not?" he challenged, his breath sweet and warm on her face. "You obviously want to stay, and you already said you'd be my mistress. Why not marry me, instead? This way you get the whole loaf, and there won't be any stigma attached to your name."

Molly stared into his eyes, trying to gauge his emotions. What was he up to? Since he held all the cards, why ask her to marry him?

"It works fine for me, but what about you? What would you get out of this marriage?"

He brushed his thumb across her bottom lip in a sweet caress. "You know what I'm going to get."

His deep voice quivered along Molly's sensitive nerve endings. His meaning was crystal clear. An undeniable excitement filled her... along with an undeniable anger at his presumptuousness. She jerked her chin free of his hold.

"Come on, Garrett," she taunted. "You're a man of the world. You don't marry someone because you want to sleep with them. There has to be something more." As soon as she'd said it, she could have bitten off her tongue. Would he think she was looking for some sign that he cared?

"Well, I sure as hell don't believe in that overrated emotion called love," he told her. "Love is nothing but raw sex accompanied by guilt. So don't expect to hear poetic words from me."

Molly shook her head in disbelief and sadness. "What happened to you, Garrett? What made you so hard? What happened to the Garrett I remember?"

"He died, Molly. A casualty of that love you still believe in."

She wished he would tell her exactly what had happened, but knew he wouldn't. She wondered if she would ever know, but if the implacable set of his jaw was any sign, she doubted she ever would. "It's fine with me if you want to grow old and bitter and give up on the human race, but don't you think there should at least be some sort of mutual respect in marriage?"

The anger in his eyes softened. "I do respect you," he told her, "for a lot of reasons. Mostly for your grit and determination to hold on to this place."

The sincerity in his eyes and voice couldn't be denied. She felt a sort of perverse pleasure in knowing that he respected her for the very thing they were at odds over.

"Finding a woman who's loyal to anything is rare these days. And, regardless of how I feel about love, I still believe in marriage for other reasons."

Molly wondered if the disillusionment she heard in his voice was real or imagined. "What other reason can their be for marriage?" she asked.

"Reasons like ours," he said logically. "Practical reasons. It will be a convenient arrangement for us both."

She rubbed at her temple, where a nagging pain throbbed with the erratic beating of her heart. "Marriages of convenience went out with whalebone corsets, Garrett."

He shrugged. "Maybe so. But you can't deny that they served a purpose, or that they sometimes worked."

She couldn't argue with that. Still, she didn't understand. "Okay, let's say I buy into that. Why marry me?" *When it's obvious you despise me and my family.*

"I don't blame you for what Liz did," he said as if he could read her mind, "but on the other hand, I don't trust you, either—not you or any other woman. Since I don't believe in love, it seems that to marry someone who cares for the same things I do is about as good as I can hope to do."

"That's interesting reasoning, but what happens if we come to hate each other?"

"Then we get a divorce," he said flatly. "And I get the plantation. Unlike my father, I'm not blinded by love. You realize of course, that there will be a prenuptial agreement."

"Of course," she mocked. She raked her hands through her hair and tried to make some sense of what was happening. Always the romantic, always searching for the rainbow, she never imagined that she'd ever consider anything as ridiculous as Garrett's proposal.

Marriage was something she hoped would happen at some time in the future, but she'd been so busy getting through her everyday life, that she hadn't had time to look for love, and it certainly hadn't walked through the plantation doors...not until the night Garrett had come back, anyway. And, as was her usual luck, it looked as if her love was destined to be one-sided. She consoled herself with the thought that even though he claimed he'd never love her, he would be sharing her bed. Maybe she could convince herself that he loved her...at least while they were making love, and if they had children...

Children. She'd always wanted them, always dreamed of having at least two. Would Garrett want to have children with her—the daughter of the woman who'd stolen his inheritance—or would she be forced to abandon that dream, too?

Molly raised her troubled eyes to his. "What about children? I've always wanted a baby."

"I'd like to have a son," he confessed.

"I didn't know if you'd want to have a child with me or not."

"I think we'd have beautiful children," he told her. "But if you do have my child, I'll never let you go."

Molly stared at him in disbelief. Realistically, she knew she could get out of a marriage, but the determined look in Garrett's eyes still caused her a moment's panic. "Did anyone ever tell you you're crazy?" she whispered.

"Once or twice," he admitted. "So? Are you going to marry me or not? It's my only offer."

A breeze rippled the curtains hanging at the window over the sink and ruffled Molly's deep-red hair. She brushed it aside and laughed—a laugh that hinted at desperation, at emotions stretched to the limit.

"Oh, I'm going to marry you, Garrett," she said, her full lips curving into a derisive smile. "Whether good or ill comes of this arrangement, I agree...to everything."

Through the open window the faint tinkling of the wind chimes accompanied the clear, soft sound of a young girl's laughter.

Surprised, Molly looked at Garrett to see if he'd heard it, too. The surprised look in his eyes told her he had. Molly couldn't recall hearing Silvie in ages. How long had it been, anyway?

Years.

Not since... Molly drew in a sharp breath. Ten years, to be exact. No one had heard Silvie laughing since Garrett and Jon had left.

Dear God, what had he done? Garrett asked himself as he drove back to the hotel later that morning. Had he actually proposed to Molly O'Connell? A woman he hardly knew, whose mother had taken his father for everything he had?

He couldn't believe what he was hearing when she'd offered to be his mistress. When he'd thrown the challenge at her, he'd intended it as a dare, a gauge to see just how far she would go to get what she wanted.

And he'd found out. She would do anything, and she wouldn't let anything stand in her way. He still had the strange feeling that this was different, that Molly was different from Liz. He didn't know if it was the memories he had of her as a girl, or the memory of the defiant expression in her eyes and the tilt of her chin, both daring him to think less of her.

Strangely, he didn't. He'd always known how much she loved the plantation, and, loving it himself, her willingness to go the extra mile to keep it seemed somehow in character. He knew that she had struggled to hang on to the house without asking anyone for help, and he admired that kind of determination and loyalty.

So much that you reward it with a marriage proposal?

Garrett shook his head. He still didn't know where that had come from. He was as surprised to hear his voice asking her to be his wife as Molly had been. Had he had a momentary lapse in sanity?

You want her. Admit it.

Okay, he wanted her, but as she'd pointed out, he could have had her without taking on the burden of a wife. Somehow, though, as she'd stood so proudly and defiantly before him, he'd known he couldn't let her do it. Whether it was the fact that he'd always thought she was an all right kid, despite her relationship to Liz, or the fact that he had enormous respect for her father, he had known that he couldn't keep her under his roof as his mistress.

Was he getting softer as he got older? Or, God forbid, was he developing a conscience? If he didn't watch out, he'd be like Jon in a few years, mellowed out, with all his fast living behind him and a woman who loved him at his side.

Right, an inner voice taunted. *And someone's gonna come along and give you the money to pull the plantation out of the slump it's in—gratis.*

No. The happiness Jon had found when he married Shiloh's mother the second time was rare...almost extinct. Even they knew they were fortunate to have been given a second chance. And Garrett realized his chances of ever finding that same happiness were slim.

His proposing to Molly must have been his subconscious kicking in, opting for the next best thing. If he couldn't have love—whatever that overrated, fickle and elusive emotion was—he'd settle for loyalty and dedication in his wife, two qualities that experience had proven were rare in women.

He held all the cards, and his logic told him that the arrangement should work. But the way his body reacted to Molly every time she came into a room and the memory of her temper warned him that the deck was pretty evenly stacked.

Molly's mind refused to stay focused on the columns of figures she was working on. She needed to get the plantation's ledgers ready for Garrett's inspection later that afternoon. Instead, her thoughts centered on his unlikely proposal and her more unlikely acceptance. Had she really consented to marry a man she hardly knew? And promised to have his children? The tantalizing turn of her thoughts sent the blood pulsing through her veins.

If only he weren't so handsome, she thought, her pencil poised above the neat rows of numbers. He'd changed so much. More handsome than ever, he'd grown cynical, hard. But if looks were the only yardstick used to measure a man's worth, Garrett would definitely be everything a woman could want.

Which is precisely the problem, Molly O. He's too handsome, and women—all women—think so. Including you. She sighed and leaned back in her chair, worrying the eraser of her pencil with her teeth. Was she doing the right thing? Was it worth giving up her

freedom and the hope of finding the love she somehow believed existed just to stay in a house?

"Molly?"

At the sound of her name being called, Molly turned
to see Jane standing in the doorway. The woman, fif-
tyish and plump, looked as if she'd been running her
stubby fingers through her coarse gray curls. Molly's
lips turned upward in a fond smile. "What's the
problem, Jane?"

"It's the well, again. The pressure's down."

Molly's smile vanished, and a familiar tenseness
settled in the back of her neck. "Damn!" she mut-
tered. "Not again!"

She followed Jane through the house, hoping the
problem was nothing more than the pesky fire ants—
which, for some unknown reason, were drawn to the
box that housed the electrical wires and points. Wasn't
it enough that she was paying through the nose for the
storm damages?

As she and Jane entered the kitchen, Garrett
stepped into the room.

Problems with the well vanished from Molly's mind
as she took in the breathtaking picture of Garrett's
masculinity. Since he'd come back into her life, she'd
only seen him in expensive slacks and shirts. This was
the Garrett she remembered...yet it wasn't. The old
Garrett had dressed in jeans and T-shirts, too, but the
jeans had been crisp and new back then, and the shirts
had born LSU fraternity emblems. For the life of her,
Molly couldn't remember him filling them out quite
so...well.

These jeans were washed to a pale blue-white and had a texture so soft and worn that there were ragged holes the size of her fists in the thighs, holes that revealed tantalizing glimpses of tanned flesh and crisply curling black hair. Filled with a longing to see what that hair-dusted flesh felt like, she dragged her gaze upward...over a straining, buttoned fly to a narrow waist and well-developed pectorals covered by a white pocket T-shirt that clung damply to him.

A ripple of desire skittered down her back. Virility and sex appeal fairly oozed from the man. Somehow, it was hard to imagine making love with him would be a hardship. Or a duty.

"What are you doing here?" she asked almost desperately.

Garrett frowned, a look which was fast becoming familiar. Didn't he ever smile anymore? she wondered.

"I told you I was coming back early so we could walk over the grounds before looking at the ledgers. Did you forget?"

She had. She'd been caught up in her daydreams. "I'm sorry," she said. "The books..."

Surprisingly, he smiled. A wry smile, true. But a smile, nonetheless. Paltry though it was, it robbed her of what little breath she had left.

"No one could ever accuse you of pandering to a man's ego," he said. Then, as if he only then noticed Jane, he held out his hand in greeting. "Hello. I'm Garrett Rambler."

Jane took his proffered hand and, if the confusion in her eyes and the blush staining her cheeks was any indication, her age was no barrier to the legendary Rambler charm. "I'm Jane Avery, a friend of Molly's."

"Very nice to meet you," Garrett said. Then, looking from one woman to the other, he asked, "Is something wrong? You both had a worried look when I came in."

"The well has gone out again," Molly said.

"Again?"

She nodded. "It's usually something simple. Fire ants or the points."

"I'll go check it out," Garrett said, already headed for the door. "You get the horses ready."

"Horses?"

He turned to look at her. "I thought we'd ride over the grounds."

"That would be wonderful, Garrett, but there are no horses. Mother sold them all after you left, and, as much as I'd like to have one, I haven't been able to afford the upkeep."

She could tell he was surprised. There had never been a time there hadn't been horses—usually thoroughbreds—at Rambler's Rest.

"Then we'll have to walk," he said. "I'll be right back."

Molly watched him leave the room and close the door behind him. She was filled with a keen sense of relief. Garrett was taking care of the well. She didn't have to worry about a thing, and he was right—not having to worry about it was wonderful.

"He's certainly a handsome devil," Jane said, going to the window and watching Garrett's loose-limbed, sexy gait take him across the yard. "Just like his daddy." She turned to Molly. "What's he doing here?"

Jane was an old friend, and Molly owed her the truth. "He came back to buy the plantation."

"Buy! But I didn't think you'd ever sell."

"Believe me, I wouldn't if I didn't have to," Molly said.

"But what about me? Will I still have a job?"

"If it's up to the new Mrs. Rambler, you will," Molly vowed firmly.

"He's marrying someone? How do you know my job's secure? Do you know her?"

Molly met her friend's worried blue eyes. "I know because *I'm* going to be the new Mrs. Garrett Rambler."

"This fence needs repairing," Garrett said, taking a small pad from the pocket of his T-shirt and jotting the notation down.

"I know."

"Do you know some good fence people?" he asked, his attention on the book in his hand.

"No."

The terseness of her reply arrested Garrett's attention. "What's the matter?"

Molly lifted her furious gaze to his. "We've been walking around for more than an hour, and all you've done is find fault with the things I've done." Her eyes shone with the angry tears she'd been suppressing.

"I've done the best I could with what I had, Garrett. I had a choice between keeping up the house or the land, and I chose the house. I realize we can't all be as perfect or as gifted at making a comeback as you obviously are, but you might show a little appreciation for the fact that I haven't stripped the house to the bare walls and lined my own pockets."

The outburst shocked him. He knew she had a temper to match her hair—he'd already seen it in action—but he hadn't intended his comments to be derogatory. He looked at her, wondering exactly what he'd said to set her off.

The humidity had made the hair around her face curl crazily. A fine sheen of perspiration dampened her temples and caused her cotton shirt to adhere to the swell of her breasts. Her chin was tilted to an angle a millimeter shy of haughty, and the pout on her lips begged to be kissed away.

Garrett fought the urge to do just that. Irritated with himself because he seemed to have no defense against her charms, his answer came out more abruptly than he intended it to sound.

"Sorry. I'm trying to get some idea of how much I need to spend to get things right, so I can figure out what to do from there."

"What do you mean?"

"That we can't make it on tours and dinners. I was raised here—remember? I know how much it takes to keep things going. We're going to have to find some use for the land, something that can bring in some steady money."

"Like what?"

"Cattle, maybe. Or rice and crawfish."

"Rice and crawfish? This is a sugar plantation!"

"Wrong," he corrected, his eyes hard and cold. "This used to be a sugar plantation. Crawfish growing is timely. The addition of so many Cajun dishes in restaurants across the country has increased the demand, and someone figured out that growing rice and raising crawfish is a symbiotic relationship. It's a type of farming that's really catching on."

"How big of an investment would it be?"

"That depends on how many acres we decide to put in—how many we can afford to put in," he explained. "Don't worry about it. Not now anyway. All I want you to worry about is getting things ready for the wedding."

"Getting things ready? B— but I thought we'd just go to the justice of the peace or something. I didn't think you'd want a real wedding."

Garrett's eyebrows lifted. "Of course I want a real wedding. This may not be a love match, but since it's the last time I ever plan to be the groom, I want it done right." Before Molly could voice an opinion, he added shortly, "Give me your hand."

Bristling at his commanding tone, she nonetheless obeyed.

Garrett saw the defiance in her eyes. "Settle down. I just want to give you your engagement ring," he said, holding up a sparkling circlet.

She hadn't thought about a ring, but then she'd given no thought at all to anything beyond her acceptance of marriage. Reluctantly, almost as if she was afraid that by accepting a ring from him there would be no turning back, Molly held out her hand and Garrett slipped the ring onto her finger.

"I love it," she said, holding out her hand to admire the baguette-cut emerald surrounded by diamonds.

Garrett took her hand in his and regarded the ring solemnly. "It was my mother's." He didn't offer her any explanation of why he hadn't given the ring to his first wife, or why he was giving her a ring which was bound to have some sentimental value, when the marriage they were about to enter into was nothing but a sham.

Molly would have liked to ask why, but the slow stroking of his thumb against the back of her hand robbed her of any sense but her growing awareness of him. Tremors of need quivered along her nerve endings. She drew her hand free before her trembling gave her away.

Garrett's mouth tightened. "Do you have any particular date that suits you?" Molly shook her head. "The sooner the better, then. June is just around the corner. Let's shoot for Saturday, the fifth."

"The fifth!" she cried. "That's only ten days from now!" She whirled away in exasperation and surprise and turned back as quickly. "I can't possibly put a wedding together in ten days. I have to find a dress and send out invitations and—"

Garrett reached out and grasped her upper arms. The moment he touched her, she grew still, and another, more subtle type of excitement invaded her quiescent body.

"Calm down," he said, his palms skimming up and down her arms with hypnotic slowness. "It's just a wedding. Let's keep it simple. A few friends. A preacher. A cake and some champagne for the reception, and a night at the Waverly in Houma. How does that sound?"

Molly looked up at him and admitted to herself that under different circumstances it would have sounded heavenly. The Waverly was a hotel built in the thirties and renovated a few years ago. With its marble floors and huge columns, it was a gorgeous testament to the simple elegance of the past. The thought of staying there with Garrett brought to mind all sorts of exciting scenarios, with the two of them as the star players.

"It sounds . . . good," she said, her voice a decibel above a whisper, her eyes locked to the mesmerizing blue of his.

"Good," he repeated in a low tone, his gaze dropping to her mouth.

She could almost feel the pressure of his lips against hers. Her tongue skimmed across their tingling surface.

A sound soughed from Garrett, something unintelligible, something between a sigh and a curse. The soft expulsion of breath caressed her lips a heartbeat before he jerked her into his arms and settled his mouth over hers in the kiss she'd dreamed of... and waited for half her lifetime.

The kiss was worth the wait.

His mouth was incredibly hot. And soft. Yet his kiss was firm and moist as his lips moved against hers. His tongue teased the crease of her lips, delving between the prim crevice, urging her in an elemental way to participate in the coupling of their mouths. Molly found that her usually strong will was putty when pitted against his gentle onslaught.

Her lips parted as his tongue delved deeper, her mouth accepting the heady sweetness of the invasion. He ground his mouth more tightly against hers. She moaned her pleasure while his was expressed by a low growl that seemed to emanate from his very soul.

He held her close, enveloping her in a heat that spread throughout her body, enveloping her in a security she couldn't remember ever experiencing.

The feel of his arms and his body pressed against hers and the touch of his mouth to her lips set off a montage of conflicting emotions. Hardness and strength, tempered with a wild gentleness. Recklessness and stability. And she was responding to him, to all the feelings binding them, but most of all she was responding to herself and a lifetime of neglected desires.

His hand stroked her breast almost roughly, and Molly thought she would die with pleasure. She was on fire wherever his mouth touched, wherever his hands touched. Tingling nerve endings screamed for something, anything. Her breasts were full and aching, and the tips were pebble-hard and hurting with need, she needed . . . she needed to be closer, pressed closer and tighter. She had never needed or wanted anything so badly in her life. She wanted to tear his T-shirt from his jeans and slide her hands beneath it, to undo the metal fastenings of his Levi's and touch the masculine hardness pressing so intimately against her belly, wanted to feel—it felt so good, so very good—the texture of his hair-crisped chest beneath her palms and see him naked before her . . . beside her . . . inside her. Wanted it so desperately that a sob of frustration fought its way from her throat and hung for a moment in the sultry bayou breeze. Her cry was a paltry token of the storm of feelings raging inside her.

The force of her desire was surprising . . . and appalling.

Appalling, because for the first time in her life she was tasting passion—real passion. For the first time in her life, she was being subjected to the temptations of the flesh, temptations her mother and sister had failed to overcome.

And for the first time in her life, she understood why.

Shocked by the wantonness of her behavior, Molly tore her mouth free of Garrett's and pushed at his chest so hard that she lost her balance. Understanding more than she knew he did, he steadied her, his hands a welcome weight on her shoulders. They stood in the midst of the knee-high grasses, eyes melded, hearts racing, breath rasping from oxygen-deprived lungs.

Molly didn't know what to say. Words escaped her. Coherent thought was an impossibility.

One corner of Garrett's mouth lifted in a derisive smile. He slid his thumb over the wet fullness of her bottom lip and carried his thumb to his own mouth where his tongue curled around it to lick the moisture away.

"Lagniappe," he said enigmatically before turning away and leaving her to ponder what in the world he was talking about.

Molly didn't sleep much that night, a problem she supposed she should get used to, now that Garrett was back in her life. She paced the floor; she drank a glass of milk and ate some cookies. Nothing worked. Every time she closed her eyes, she could see herself in Garrett's arms, his mouth on hers, his hand cupping her breast.

She burned with desire and shame. Not so much over her body's response, but at *whom* it had responded to. There was something depressing, if not demeaning, about feeling so aroused over a man who felt no love for her, a man who had made it as clear as he possibly could that he wanted nothing from her but the use of her body.

In desperation, Molly counted down the days until the ceremony and wondered if Garrett would expect her to make love with him on their wedding night. She'd never considered marrying for convenience's sake before, so she didn't know the rules—or if there were any. Even if she did know the etiquette, she had the feeling Garrett was the kind of man who'd throw the book away.

The next day, knowing that she had to break the news to her family soon, Molly drove to Houma to visit her father.

"Hello, sprite," Ian O'Connell said, taking her by the shoulders and giving her a brief hug. "To what do we owe the honor of your visit?"

Molly looked up into his dear face—were there more lines there than there had been the last time she came to call?—and felt the invisible fingers of guilt squeeze her heart. She never visited him and her stepmother as often as she should, but there never seemed to be enough time to do everything.

That's all changed now, Molly. Which is exactly why you're here—to break the news of your impending wedding.

Impending. The word her mind had tossed out brought a taunting smile to her lips. It was a word generally associated with doom, not weddings. Then, realizing that her father was waiting for her answer, Molly brushed his cheek with a kiss and said, "I've missed you."

"Sure, sure," he said, heading for the living room.

Molly laughed and tucked her arm in his. "The road goes both ways, you know."

Ian smiled and nodded. "So it does. Life just gets complicated sometimes, doesn't it? Have a seat. Veronica will be in shortly."

"How is Ronnie?"

"Your stepmother is fine, as I'm sure Cindy told you today. I'm also sure you know that she told me that Garrett Rambler showed up at the plantation a few days ago. He isn't giving you any trouble, is he?" Ian asked with true fatherly concern.

Molly recalled the gamut of emotions she'd experienced since Garrett's return. "Trouble" would be putting it mildly. "No," she said with a shake of her head. "Actually, he's saving me some trouble."

"Come again?"

"Garrett came back because he heard I was in over my head financially," Molly explained. "He wanted to buy Rambler's Rest and give me enough money to get into another house somewhere."

Ian raised his bushy dark eyebrows and took a pull from his Meerschaum. "That was pretty decent of him, considering what Liz did. So what are you going to do?"

"I wasn't going to accept the offer until the storm hit. It didn't leave me a choice."

"So you're selling." Ian drew on his pipe and shook his head. "Never thought I'd see the day you'd leave that place willingly. Figured they'd have to carry you out in a box. Do you—"

"I'm not leaving, Daddy."

"—have you any idea where you'll be moving?" Ian continued as if Molly hadn't spoken. "There are some nice houses for sale in this neighborhood."

"I said I'm not leaving."

The words finally sunk in. "What do you mean, you're not leaving? If Garrett buys— Oh, I see. You're going to stay on as a housekeeper or something."

"Or something," Molly agreed, rising and going to look out the window. The modest neighborhood was quiet in the heat of the day. She supposed everyone was inside keeping cool, sleeping...or idling away the day by making love.

Making love. She'd be making love with Garrett. Sleeping with him. Without warning, the memory of his kiss the day before and her response sauntered through her mind. Shame and heat suffused her body. She turned to face her father.

"Garrett has asked me to marry him, and I've accepted," she blurted out.

"What!" Ian thundered.

"Now, Daddy, calm down," she said. "It's—" she shrugged "—sort of a business arrangement. There's no man in my life who matters. Garrett doesn't believe in love. And we both care about what happens to the plantation. It makes perfect sense."

"It makes no sense!" Ian growled. "Have you forgotten what his father did to your mother?"

"Have you forgotten what she did to you?" Molly countered in desperation.

Ian's smile was bitter. "Touché, brat."

Molly crossed the room and sat down on the arm of her father's favorite chair. She put her arms around his shoulders, which sloped from hours of pouring over his beloved books. "She hurt you, Daddy. And she intended to hurt you. Mama wasn't a very nice person, but I'm not her, and Garrett isn't Jon."

"Thank God," Ian said, giving her a fierce hug. He looked up into her eyes. "I want you to be happy."

She shrugged off the idea of happiness. "Garrett and I are going into this with our eyes open."

"What about love? Despite what Liz's actions may have taught you, it is a valid emotion. Ronnie and I can testify to that."

"I know," she whispered, pushing back a strand of his thinning hair and remembering how Veronica's love had healed the wounds Liz had inflicted. She blinked rapidly and tried to smile. "It'll be all right, Daddy."

"He'll break your heart," he said, reaching up and wiping at an errant tear with his fingertip.

His gentleness and the truth of his warning destroyed the last bit of her resistance, and the tears she'd been holding back finally tumbled over the fragile barrier of her lower lashes. Nodding, she leaned her face against his cheek and let her tears fall.

"I know."

Chapter Five

Garrett spent the two days following the kiss in Baton Rouge, trying, with some success, to find out all he could about starting up the rice and crawfish venture, but failing miserably to forget the feel of Molly in his arms. While in the capitol, he called his father and broke the news of his marriage. Jon was less than happy.

Hoping for support from any quarter, he called his half sister, Shiloh, who likewise hit the ceiling.

"I thought you liked Molly," Garrett said.

"I liked her fine as a girl," Shiloh specified. "But she's a woman now. And she's Liz's daughter.

"She isn't like Liz, sis. If she was, she'd have sold the place for what she could get long before now. But she hasn't. It means a lot to her, and I hate to see her kicked out onto the street, so to speak.''

Shiloh laughed, a low, sexy sound that invariably attracted men. ''My, my, my. You actually feel sorry for her. Don't tell me my big brother has developed a conscience?''

The fact that Shiloh's reasoning so closely coincided with his infuriated Garrett, but for the life of him he didn't know why. ''I don't feel sorry for her.''

Shiloh sighed. ''Then why are you marrying her, Garrett? You swore you'd never marry again after Lacey.''

Garrett heard the genuine concern in his sister's voice. ''I'm tired of being alone.''

There was a long pause. ''As a spinster in a marry-now-divorce-later world, I can relate to that, but, Garrett, loneliness is a pretty shallow reason to marry someone.''

''I know that. Actually, there are a couple of others.''

''Ah,'' Shiloh said, the teasing note back in her voice, ''those nasty little critters—sex and sex, right? Sorry, big guy, but that isn't a good basis for a marriage, either.''

''Will you shut up and let me finish?'' Garrett said with exasperation. Shiloh, it seemed, knew him better than he thought. ''Sex is part of it,'' he agreed. ''Molly has grown into an extremely beautiful, desirable woman.'' He didn't tell his sister about Molly's offer to become his mistress. For some reason he didn't want Shiloh to think less of Molly.

"The biggest reason I asked her to marry me is that I want a family."

Silence followed his announcement. "You never seemed like the type who wanted to perpetuate the species," she quipped.

"It isn't that. I want someone to love me in spite of what I've done, maybe even in spite of who I am. You and I have learned that the relationship between child and parent is about as close to that as it comes."

"What can I say?" she said. "You're right. Even during those years Dad and Mother were divorced and after he married Liz, he was still just Dad. Funny and loving and warm."

Garrett couldn't fail to notice the wistfulness in Shiloh's voice. "Thank God they got back together," he said.

Shiloh sighed deeply. "Yeah." She paused. "So, why pick Molly as a mother for your kids?"

"It's hard to find anyone who has any staying power or who is willing to commit to anything these days, and Molly is one of those rare few who can commit. She hung on and fought the world—including me—to keep what she felt was hers. That, and the fact that she's willing to go into this marriage and stay married—for whatever reason—is cause enough for me to give it a try."

"And you don't have the entanglement of love."

"What Molly and I have agreed to will last a lot longer than that fickle emotion called love."

Shiloh sighed again. "Maybe you're right," she said. "Maybe it will."

* * *

"There's no way I can make a wedding dress in a week!" Veronica O'Connell fumed.

"I know it's a lot to ask, but—" Molly's explanation was interrupted by the ringing of the kitchen phone. She brushed aside a tendril of hair and reached for the receiver. "Rambler's Rest."

When the caller identified herself as the social columnist of a local paper, Molly grimaced. Gossip columnist would be a more accurate description, she thought. Mavis Davenport was the biggest gossip monger from Baton Rouge to New Orleans. Great.

"Hello, Mavis," Molly said, determined to get the woman off the phone as soon as decency allowed. "Yes, it's true. I am marrying Garrett Rambler. How did you find out? Oh. I forgot the paper prints the names of the marriage license applicants."

She paused. "The date is set for the fifth of June. I'm sorry. Family and close friends only. No press. No, I don't have any comment. Yes, I understand that the marriage is hot news under the circumstances, but I don't think anyone is entitled to a blow-by-blow account of either of our lives, regardless of the scandal surrounding our parents."

Molly cast a glance at her stepmother who made a slashing motion across her throat. Molly struggled to control a smile and rolled her eyes. "Yes, Mavis," she said patiently, "I know the Ramblers are one of the oldest families in the area and anything they do is news, but I'm not a Rambler yet— You're right, there has been a lot between us. Yes, we do go back a long way, but— Look," she said, when it became obvious that Mavis planned on doing all the talking, "Why don't you talk with Garrett? Oh. Well, that's that, then. I'm sorry. Goodbye."

She cradled the receiver none too gently and looked at Veronica in exasperation. "That woman is a barracuda."

Veronica grimaced. "You're being too kind. I can't wait to see what she puts in the paper."

Molly frowned. "What can she put? I refused to tell her anything. I told her to talk to Garrett, but evidently he wouldn't talk to her, either."

"Good for him," Molly's stepmother said. "Still, the woman has a very creative mind, and she always gets in her two cents' worth."

The phone rang again, and Molly threw up her hands in frustration. "How am I supposed to plan a wedding when the phone keeps ringing?"

She snatched the receiver up. "Hello," she snapped.

"This is Garrett," he said without a word of greeting. "I called to tell you—"

"Hello, Garrett," Molly interrupted with saccharine sweetness. "My day has been a disaster. Thanks for asking."

There was a lengthy pause on the line while Garrett mulled over what she'd said. "I've been busy and..." His voice trailed away. "Never mind," he said. "Being busy is no excuse for rudeness."

"Your apology is accepted," Molly said, knowing that what he'd said was as close as she was going to get to an "I'm sorry."

"I called to tell you that you can expect a call from Mavis Davenport."

"She's already called."

Garrett swore. "The woman is fast. And a bloodsucker. What did you tell her?"

"That the wedding was for family and close friends only and to call you. She said she had, and I hung up."

"Good." Silence stretched between them. "You said your day was a disaster. What happened?"

"I had a fight with the caterer, the printer is charging me an arm and a leg to put a rush on the invitations, I can't find a dress, and Veronica says she can't possibly make one in time. And it's barely noon."

"Why don't you forget the invitations, since it's family and friends? You call yours. I'll call mine. Fair enough?"

"Yes, but I thought you'd want things to be . . . just so," she said.

"As long as the preacher's there, I don't care about the rest."

His attitude came as a complete surprise. "Thanks, then. I'll call and cancel."

"Had you thought about using Lisette's dress?" Garrett suggested out of the blue.

"Lisette's dress?" Molly said. Why hadn't she thought of that? "I'd love to, but didn't Jon donate it to the Louisiana Historical Society Museum?"

"He did, but he hired that woman from Natchitoches to make a replica of it first. I think it's packed away in the attic somewhere."

Molly brightened. "I'll go look." A sudden thought dimmed her happiness. "How do I know I can wear it?"

"You're small. So was she. Maybe Veronica can do some alterations," he suggested.

"But what about you?"

"I had a suit like Nate's made for Mardi Gras one year. I'll wear it."

Molly's mind raced ahead, picturing Garrett as he might have looked a hundred years ago: better than wonderful. Wearing a period wedding dress and saying the wedding vows to Garrett in the English garden would be the perfect realization of her childhood dreams. Again she was touched by his thoughtfulness—or was it his practicality? Either way, Molly was glad for the truce in the ongoing battle between them. "I'm sure she can. Thanks, Garrett," she said softly. "I'd love to wear Lisette's dress.

They hung up soon after, and, together, Molly and Veronica climbed the attic stairs and rummaged around until they found what they were looking for. Inside a steamer trunk, swaddled in white sheets, was the replica of Lisette's dress. Filled with a growing excitement, Molly cradled the dress reverently in her arms and carried it downstairs.

With Veronica's help, she tried the gown on and, with a blush of pleasure coloring her cheeks, she turned this way and that in front of the cheval mirror in her room. Veronica was reduced to oohs and aahs.

Made of white silk with a voluminous skirt gathered to a form-fitting, deep vee waist, the dress enhanced Molly's natural slenderness. The skirt was gathered up in places by pale-pink bows to reveal a frilly underskirt that boasted row after row of tiny lace ruffles. The three-quarter length sleeves ended in a three-inch lace ruffle. The bodice was close-fitting, pushing her breasts upward and baring her shoulders.

A hot breeze blew through the open window, fluttering the lacy trim. From across the hallway and through the open doors came the sound of wind chimes dancing in the wind.

Molly adjusted the double flounces that revealed a generous portion of the upper part of her breasts, never so thankful as now that she was one of those rare creatures—a redhead without so much as a freckle. Smiling with pleasure, she fluffed the loose ruffles and straightened the cluster of pink satin roses nestling between her breasts. Exquisitely feminine, the wedding dress was everything it should be.

A sobering thought dampened her enthusiasm and brought an ache to her heart. Wearing the dress that symbolized the happiness that Nate and Lisette shared was nothing short of a sham. She wondered what Lisette would think if she knew her dress was being used in a marriage that wasn't sanctioned by love?

"What do you think, Silvie?"

"What did you say?" Veronica asked.

Startled and embarrassed that she'd been caught talking to a ghost, Molly turned away. "Nothing," she said. "I was just talking to myself."

Outside, the wind chimes jangled joyously.

* * *

"What the hell is the meaning of this?" Garrett growled, entering the kitchen later that afternoon with a newspaper held up in the air. He stopped dead in his tracks when he saw Molly standing at the sink, tearing lettuce for a salad, clad in tight biker's pants and a short T-shirt that exposed a generous portion of her midriff. The spandex clung lovingly to the sweet curve of her bottom and the slender length of her thighs.

"What's what?" Molly asked, glancing at him over her shoulder. Her first thought was that he looked absolutely wonderful in his pleated slacks and pearl-gray dress shirt. The second was that their truce hadn't lasted long at all.

Garrett smacked the newspaper against the palm of his hand. "I'm talking about this article by Mavis Davenport. What did you tell her?"

"Nothing," Molly said, wiping her hands on her apron. She sighed.

"She didn't come up with all this garbage from nothing."

Molly didn't intend to let Garrett run roughshod over her. She jerked the paper out of his hands and opened it. "I told you what I said to her."

Without waiting for his answer, her greedy gaze zeroed in on the story which comprised a major portion of the first page of the social section.

There was a picture of Liz and Jon, taken as they came out of the courtroom, and one of Garrett taken the year he'd announced his engagement to Lacey. Molly even found a snapshot of herself standing on the steps of the house, taken by a newspaper photographer when she first started doing dinner parties.

While Garrett's eyes skimmed her body, Molly's skimmed the article, which started by rehashing Liz's and Jon's divorce. Then, Mavis mentioned Liz's death and hinted at Molly's financial problems. Shock and amazement at the columnist's gall rose with every printed word Molly read.

Mavis made Molly's reluctance to answer questions about the marriage seem churlish and snobbish and Garrett's refusal sound cloaked with mystery. The way she twisted what few innocent comments Molly had made was unbelievable. She read on, her fury growing.

Mavis refreshed everyone's memory about how long the plantation had belonged to the Ramblers and how everyone knew how much their heritage meant to them. The lowest blow came when she referred to Molly's comment about there being a great deal between her and Garrett and the fact that they went back a long way. Mavis had used a generous amount of journalistic license so that it came across as the thinly-veiled cause of the breakup of Garrett's marriage a year before. Mavis slyly conjectured that Garrett had dumped his wife and was marrying Molly just to regain control of his legacy.

Even though it was partially true, it hurt...as did the reminder that this wasn't Garrett's first foray down the path of matrimony.

Molly straightened her shoulders and threw the paper onto the table. The look in her eyes dared him to place the blame on her. "I didn't say anything to make her think there was anything going on between us. If you'll reread it, you'll see that the last sentence negates her allegation that I was the cause of your breakup with Lacey."

Damn, but she was gorgeous when she was riled, Garrett thought. He wondered randomly if that was one of the reasons he kept her stirred up all the time. He picked up the paper and read the last few sentences. Then he laid it back down and shoved his hands into his pockets. He had the grace to look embarrassed.

"Evidently, you haven't heard about Mavis Davenport."

"No," Garrett said with a shake of his head.

Molly smiled, a wry twisting of her full lips. "Suffice it to say that everything that anyone of social standing in the area says or does is grist for her mill."

"I know the type," Garrett said shortly. "I'll keep that in mind."

Touched by his apparent regret over his earlier hostility and not wanting to fight with him, Molly eyed the briefcase sitting near his feet. "Did you and Mac get everything taken care of?"

He nodded. "All we have to do is go in tomorrow and sign the papers. I put the money I was going to give you into a special account. You can do what you like with it."

"I didn't expect you to do that," she said. "You aren't buying the plantation from me, so it isn't the same situation at all."

Garrett hooked his index finger over the knot of his tie and worked it loose. "Think of it as insurance," he told her, undoing the top two buttons of his shirt.

Or a payoff. "In case the marriage doesn't work," she said, just to make sure she knew where they stood.

"They've been known not to," was his enigmatic reply.

"Like yours and Lacey's?"

Garrett was halfway to the credenza where Molly kept a decanter of brandy. The question was directed to his back. He turned and looked at her, surprise and anger evident in the depths of his blue eyes.

"Not that it's any of your business, but, yeah, like mine and Lacey's."

"I beg your pardon," Molly said, "but I think it's very much my business." The look in his eyes warned her to back off, but angry with her or not, as the next Mrs. Rambler, she felt he owed her some explanation. She deliberately softened the belligerent tone in her voice. "Please. I'd like to know."

Garrett's eyes were gemstone hard. He moved his head up and down in a slow nod. "I guess you're right. You do have a right to know." He sauntered the rest of the way to the credenza and poured his drink. Turning, he lifted it in a mock salute. "To us."

He took a healthy swallow, grimaced and swore. For long moments, he stood there, swirling the liquor round and round in the glass. When he lifted his head, there was a coldness in his eyes that sent a shiver down Molly's spine. "It was the casino."

"What?"

He took another sip of his drink. "She married me because she had this addiction—to gambling. I thought she was in love with me, but what she was in love with was the fact that she could gamble from daylight 'til dark." He smiled, a lopsided, weary sort of smile that caused the crease in his left cheek to appear more prominent.

"It was a mortal blow to my ego when I found out she was seeing one of the croupiers on the side. I divorced her as fast as the law would allow. You might remember, Molly, that I don't like to share what's mine. And I'll fight to keep it to the bitter end."

"Then why did you let her go?" Molly asked, needing to understand so that she might understand him better. "Why didn't you fight for her?"

"Because I knew she'd never been mine and that I was better off without her." His eyes bored into hers. "Let me give you a friendly word of advice. Don't ever fool around on me."

"I'm not that kind of woman," Molly said, aghast at the thought.

He swallowed the last of the brandy. "That's what she said." Before Molly had a chance to respond, he added, "Hey, it's no big deal. But now you know why I don't intend to fall for the I-love-you ploy anymore."

As Liz's daughter, Molly did understand.

"Enough of that," Garrett said, pouring himself another drink. "How did the rest of your day go? Did you find the dress?"

Molly struggled to put his confession behind her and focus on the new tack the conversation had taken. She plastered a smile on her face and tried to appear excited. "Yes. It's a gorgeous dress, and Veronica isn't going to have to do much to alter it at all."

Garrett couldn't help noticing how animated Molly's features became when she talked about the wedding. Knowing that she would soon be the mistress of Rambler's Rest had erased the worry from her eyes and lit them with a sparkle of happiness and excitement. For an instant, he realized that this marriage was something of a parallel to his previous marriage. After all, in each case, he had something they both wanted.

"And if the weather holds..."

Making another leisurely survey of Molly's body, he thought that maybe he should just forget it—buy her out, and kick her out. But he knew he wouldn't. She had something he wanted, too. But it was more than that. The same instinct that told him when he had a good hand of cards or when to trust another throw of the dice told him that he'd be a fool to let Molly get away. After all the times he'd seen women make fools of men, he didn't know why he trusted that inner voice, but he realized he did.

"Garrett?" Molly's voice intruded on his troubled thoughts.

Startled into awareness, he glanced at her. "Yes?"

"Is everything all right?"

Garrett tried to remember what she'd just said. A twinge of irritation made his voice gruff. "I'm sorry.

I was thinking about something. You're right. We'll have to hope for good weather. Did you call the Waverly?''

"The Waverly?"

He nodded. "To make reservations for our honeymoon."

Molly's heart faltered at the thought of sharing a room—a bed—with him. If he loved her it would be different. If he loved her it would be a cause for celebration. "No. Look, Garrett, I—"

"You're not backing out, are you?"

"No."

"Good. Don't forget that this is a mutually beneficial arrangement." His voice sounded cold and impersonal, and he tried not to notice how pale Molly suddenly grew. He tried not to think about what a bastard he was. Instead, he forced himself to concentrate on his own past heartaches and the ways he could protect himself from experiencing any more of the same. "So is tomorrow okay to sign the papers?" he asked.

To her credit, she didn't bat an eyelash. In a familiar and strangely endearing gesture that told him she was ready to do battle, she lifted her chin and met his unflinching gaze. "Tomorrow's fine," she said, turning to leave the room.

"Where are you going?"

Molly looked at him over her shoulder, her eyes filled with a remarkable steadiness. "To call the Waverly."

Garrett watched her go. Though he couldn't help admiring her composure and the gentle sway of her hips, he still heard her voice chanting: *I'll get the money somehow. I'd sell myself... Sell myself...*

It was almost painless. Almost. Molly carefully laid the pen on Mac Henning's desk and sat back in the leather armchair. Garrett and the notary signed next, and, just like that, she'd signed away all her rights to Rambler's Rest. Molly let the conversation flow on around her while she pondered the seriousness of what she was doing.

She had to admit that in the event their marriage failed, Garrett's generosity couldn't be faulted. But somehow, all the things he promised seemed like nothing compared to what she was giving up. She felt a bitter smile tugging at one corner of her mouth. Of course, it wouldn't have been hers much longer anyway. Half a loaf was better than none as the old saying went, and the secret was, of course, not to let the marriage fail.

Which she suspected might be easier said than done. Ever since their talk the day before, Garrett had been withdrawn, unapproachable. She told herself that it was the memory of his other marriage that had made him so taciturn, but she couldn't help wondering how it would be to live with a brooding stranger day after day. And she wondered if there was any chance of changing him in the future.

You can't change a person, Molly. Ian's voice, spouting one of his favorite platitudes, flashed through her mind. He'd been talking about Liz and Krystal, but Molly knew the advice could be applied to anyone ... even Garrett. Especially Garrett.

"Congratulations, Molly my dear," Mac Henning boomed, the sound of his voice jolting her out of her somber thoughts. "I think you've made a wise decision."

Molly stifled the urge to call the pudgy banker a hypocrite. After the little scene he'd witnessed between her and Garrett and her determination not to sell the plantation to him, Henning must know that they weren't the usual lovestruck couple. He had to know that congratulations had nothing to do with their strange alliance. Nonetheless, she forced a half smile to her lips. "Thank you."

Garrett helped Molly to her feet, and the two men shook hands. Then, with his hand resting at the small of her back, Garrett ushered her to the door. "I'll be in touch about the rice irrigation project," he said, "just as soon as we get the wedding behind us and I can get the figures in."

"Good, good," Henning said. His smile pushed his cheeks upward until his eyes were mere slits in his shiny face. "I'll be looking forward to it."

Molly managed to bite her tongue until she and Garrett had left the building. Turning to him, she lifted her hand to shield her eyes from the glare of the afternoon sun. "You're still planning on going through with the rice and crawfish thing, then?"

Garrett unlocked the car door and opened it for her. He nodded. "Yes. I thought you understood that."

Molly sat down on the edge of the car seat and looked up at him. "I don't like it."

"Why?"

"It's too new, too risky."

"No guts, no glory."

"Maybe so, but I don't like it. Why can't we just put in some coastal or something that won't require so much outlay?"

Garrett closed the door and, rounding the front of the car, got in on his side. There was a hint of irritation in his eyes. "Because that won't bring in nearly the money the crawfish and rice will."

"And is money the be-all and end-all to your existence?"

He started the car and gave her a scathing sideways look. "I like having enough so that I don't have to worry about paying my bills."

"How do you propose to finance this venture?"

"I'm not sure," he confessed. "I'm still working on that. Mac says we'll need some collateral, and I'm not about to put the plantation up again. Not when I've just spent every cent I have on getting it out of hock."

A sigh of relief fluttered from Molly's lips. Thank goodness! She was tired of worrying about whether or not she'd have someplace to lay down her head.

"Actually, I was thinking of using the paintings as collateral."

"The paintings?" she echoed. "You don't mean the Landseer and Bonheur?"

"Of course I mean the Landseer and Bonheur. What other paintings do we have that are worth anything?"

"But they're priceless!"

"Not exactly priceless. Expensive on today's market, but not priceless."

"No."

"What do you mean, no?" Garrett asked.

"I won't let you do it," she told him firmly.

"*You* won't let me do it?" he said, and the tone of his voice and the look in his eyes reminded her that she had no say now in what he did with the plantation or its furnishings.

The enormity of what she had done swept through her like the hurricanes that periodically swept the Louisiana shores. She had no rights, no say. Once she was married to Garrett, she would be nothing but his chattel. She felt a painful tightening in her throat.

"So that's the way it's going to be." It was a statement, not a question.

Garrett swore, violently. It wasn't the way he wanted it. He'd never intended to be the sole decision-maker but he didn't intend to let Molly talk him out of something he felt was right, either.

"Yes, dammit, that's the way it's going to be. If you agree with me, fine. If not, that's fine, too. I want to secure the future of the plantation, and this is the most viable plan I've been able to come up with. Rice and crawfish are hot commodities, and we have the bayou nearby to use for irrigation. It's a perfect setup."

Molly couldn't deny that the plan made sense, but... "But to put up the paintings..." Her voice trailed away. "They're a part of the house, a part of your heritage."

"I realize that, but I have to take a chance. Otherwise I'll soon be in the same shape you were in. Rambler's Rest is a monster that gobbles up money like crazy."

She didn't answer. Garrett regarded her stubborn profile for an instant before he returned his attention to the road. He couldn't help feeling a reluctant admiration for her. How could he be angry at her for displaying the very tenacity he was marrying her for? He felt his heart and his manner soften, and called himself a fool for allowing her to get to him.

"You're a tough lady, Molly O'Connell. Lucky for you, it's too late to plant this year, anyway. I need to have my financing worked out before next spring, but I suppose the least I can do is check into some alternatives."

Molly turned to look at him. She knew that this concession to her wishes hadn't been easy for him to make. Somehow, she knew she'd won a major victory. "Thank you, Garrett," she said, once again, touched by his actions.

"Sure."

They drove for a few moments in silence, and before they knew it, they were approaching the crushed-shell driveway of Rambler's Rest. As always, when she saw it, Molly felt a sense of homecoming. As a child, she'd welcomed it. As an adult, she understood that the house represented the only permanence in her young life. A permanence and feeling of belonging she hadn't always enjoyed because of the transient lifestyle engendered by Liz's climb to the top. They were feelings she didn't want to give up.

"I always feel like I'm coming home," Garrett said, his words a counterpart to her thoughts.

Molly sighed in defeat. They both belonged here. They both understood the pull of the plantation, and they would both do anything to maintain the ties they felt. If she had had any doubts about committing herself to this marriage, they vanished with his words. No matter what happened, or how stormy her future might be, she knew that what she and Garrett were about to do was as inevitable as the setting of the sun.

"I know," she said, and the two simple words seemed like the sealing of her fate.

Chapter Six

On the day of the wedding, Molly paced the floor and wondered what in the world she was doing marrying a man who looked at her as if he'd like to drag her off into the bushes, a man who, so far, had few kind words to say. In an effort to calm her sudden bout of nerves, she donned a faded seersucker robe over her strapless bra and French-cut panties and wandered out onto the back gallery to give the garden one final look. She suspected Garrett would settle for nothing but perfection, even though he maintained it was only a wedding.

At least the weather was being cooperative. The June afternoon was warm and balmy with a slight breeze that blew marshmallow-crème clouds across the blue sky and made the wind chimes play a gentle song. Even the humidity was at an acceptable level.

The garden was a riot of color, from the deep-green ivy climbing the massive trunks of the oak trees to the caladiums bordering the house to the roses that bloomed in every conceivable color. Chairs faced the center of the rose garden where an ancient, white lattice arbor dripped scarlet roses. A sundial marked the descent of the setting sun and, on either side of the arbor, Boston ferns sat on marble-topped stands. Each was adorned with a pink satin bow whose streamers trickled onto the close-cropped St. Augustine.

More roses and ivy spilled over the lip of a large silver vase and onto a creamy, white damask cloth. A silver coffee service, delicate crystal cups and Spode dessert plates sat waiting for the arrival of the tiered wedding cake. A crystal punch bowl meant to be filled with pink champagne completed the arrangement.

Looking down at the setting, Molly felt that it was nicely done for the short notice she'd had. And, even though she'd objected, Ian had paid for everything. After all, he'd said with a glimmer of tears in his eyes, it wasn't every day his eldest daughter got married.

Molly had seen the question in her father's eyes, even as he'd said it. Was she sure she was doing the right thing? And would the marriage last? Even though she was dedicated to going through with it, Molly wondered, as well.

No, she chided herself sternly, reaching up to toy with the tiny brass bells of the wind chimes, that was the wrong attitude to have on the day of her wedding.

She should have determination and faith. She sighed and dropped her hand to her side. The determination was no problem. But faith, considering the circumstances, was a little harder to come by. Faith was difficult to scare up when she knew that she held no place in Garrett's heart . . . and that, according to him, she never would.

Over the past week, she'd reconciled herself to the fact that her feelings for Garrett had only grown and changed through the years; they had not died. And, as much as it frightened her to think of giving her body to a virtual stranger, there was a certain satisfaction—even a frightening sense of excitement—in knowing that he wanted her. If she hoped to find any happiness or any contentment in her marriage she would have to give it everything she had and pray that Garrett might not only participate in the physical side of love but might eventually give a bit of his heart away.

"What do you think, Silvie?" Molly asked, grasping the railing and lifting her face to the sky. "Am I crazy? Should I forget this whole scheme?"

"Who are you talking to?"

The voice—unmistakably Garrett's—came from below her. Molly leaned over the parapet. There, resplendent in his wedding finery, a thin cigar in his hand, stood Garrett. A wave of dizziness that had nothing to do with heights, swept over her.

He was gorgeous. And dangerous-looking. A Nathan Rambler, riverboat gambler look-alike. His shirt was pristine white, and his black pants fit snugly across his hips. His black coat was pinstripe, and someone had already pinned a boutonniere to his lapel. The striking ensemble was accentuated by shiny leather boots, a white silk handkerchief that peeked from his breast pocket and a perfectly tied ebony cravat complete with pearl stickpin.

Funny, even though there was a breeze, she felt suffocated. "What?" she said breathlessly, in answer to his question . . . which she'd already forgotten.

"I asked who you were talking to."

How could she tell him that, like Aunt Lisbet, she talked to ghosts? "No one," she said with a shake of her head. "Just myself."

"Second thoughts?" he ventured, with a mocking lift of his heavy eyebrows.

"A few," she answered honestly.

"Just think of it as a business venture . . . a merger," he suggested. "Or another step toward attaining a goal. After all, isn't that what it is? We're both going into this to get something we want."

Molly didn't like the reckless gleam in his blue eyes . . . or his subtle reference to sex. He was right. If she could keep things between them on an impersonal level . . .

How do you keep things impersonal if you're sharing a bed? a niggling voice inside her asked. Feeling uncomfortable, she angled her chin upward. She'd die before she let him know how apprehensive she was.

"Yes," she agreed, "I guess we are."

"Garrett! Who are you talking to?"

Cindy, wearing a frilly pink bridesmaid dress and a wide smile, swept out onto the gallery.

"Your sister," he told her.

Cindy's smile disappeared. Twisting around, she looked up and saw Molly looking down at them. "Molly! What are you doing out here talking to him?" She pinned Garrett with a stern look. "You know you aren't supposed to see the bride until the ceremony."

"I'm sorry, sweetheart," Garrett told Cindy with a smile. "I was smoking, and she just happened to be there."

"Well, you can just get back inside. Better yet," she said, craning her neck upward, "Molly, you get inside. You aren't even dressed yet, and the wedding is supposed to start in thirty minutes."

Sadness filled Molly's heart. The smile he'd given Cindy was one she remembered all too well as a means to capture unsuspecting hearts. And it wasn't one that he'd given her since he'd come back. Cindy, with the often shortsightedness and hopefulness of youth, refused to look at the wedding of her half sister and the man Liz had wronged as anything but "totally" romantic.

Molly sighed. "If you'll help me into my dress, I'll be ready in a jiffy."

"I'm coming right up," Cindy promised. She looked at Garrett and placed one rose-tipped finger in the center of his wide chest. "Inside."

"Yes, ma'am. In just a minute."

Cindy flounced away, and, with a smile that looked almost sad, Garrett watched her go. "Pretty girl," he said at last.

"She has a crush on you," Molly said, hoping the news would serve as a warning to treat Cindy gently in the future, no matter what his relationship with his wife might be.

"Then maybe I'm marrying the wrong sister," he said somberly.

"Maybe you are," she volleyed back. "But, even if she were old enough, I'm afraid her nonstop talking might drive you crazy."

Garrett's gaze caressed her face and dropped to her breasts. There was a sudden heat in his eyes that Molly understood too well. "You drive me crazy," he said, and, turning, left her standing there, confusion in her eyes, and a frightening combination of fear and exhilaration filling her heart.

The minister's words were a faraway hum. *"You drive me crazy."*

Trembling, Molly watched Garrett slip the plain gold wedding band on her finger and then looked up at him from beneath her lashes. The look on his face was familiar. Serious and...almost angry. *"Crazy..."*

She didn't hear the preacher pronounce them man and wife, but she saw Garrett take the hem of her veil and lift it over her head. It was almost over, she thought. There was just the kiss....

And the night.

She felt his arms draw her close, and his lips touched hers sweetly, gently. Lightheaded, Molly clung to him, parting her lips for the brief, perfunctory touching of their mouths. Garrett released her from the kiss and, clinging to each other, they faced the beaming preacher once more.

"Congratulations," he said with a smile. Then, indicating that they should face their guests, he said, "Ladies and gentlemen, may I present Mr. and Mrs. Jonathan Garrett Rambler."

In spite of everything, Molly thought an hour later, it felt like a real wedding. Though Jon and Ellen hadn't been able to make it, Shiloh had driven down from Tennessee, bringing a mountain of gifts. Cindy caught the bridal bouquet, and Veronica's nephew caught the garter. A friend of Ian's had captured the entire ceremony on video cassette, and Ian snapped furiously with his 35mm during the reception. Everyone laughed and joked and toasted the newlyweds. It was almost as if her family thought that if they pretended it were a normal wedding it would somehow miraculously become one.

Molly cast a quick glance at Garrett, who sat at her side on the gallery, helping her open wedding gifts. They were both great actors, she thought. He was the picture of the happy groom, keeping her close at his side, his arm around her waist as they chatted with friends and family. Knowing that her moment of reckoning would come eventually, Molly had thrown herself into the charade, too. The look on Garrett's face told her he knew she was playing the part for the benefit of their guests.

Molly was opening a card while Garrett wrestled with a particularly stubborn package. In exasperation, he reached for the scissors and cut the ribbon. Giggles from the ladies rippled throughout the gallery.

"You shouldn't have done that," Cindy said.

"Why?" he asked, looking from Molly to her younger sister.

"Every ribbon you deliberately cut is a baby."

"Oh," Garrett said, for once at a loss for words. "I didn't know," he said to Cindy. "What if it was an accident?"

"It doesn't matter."

He shrugged and looked at Molly who looked back at him innocently. "I'll just have to be careful from now on," he said, but his eyes plainly told Molly that careful or not, he'd like to be doing something wickedly wonderful to her at that very moment.

"Hey, you two," Shiloh said in her soft Tennessee drawl, "save that stuff for the hotel."

"Stuff it, Shiloh," Garrett said as the phone rang. He answered it on the second ring and held the receiver out to Molly.

"It's for you." His face, which had worn a look of desire only moments before, now looked grim, closed.

Apprehension trickled down her spine. "Who is it?"

Garrett shook his head.

"I'll take it inside," she said, her gaze bouncing off his. He nodded, and Molly went in, oblivious to the concerned looks on the faces of her guests. Her hand trembled as she picked up the receiver, but for the life of her she didn't know why. "Hello." She heard a click and realized Garrett had hung up the other phone.

"Hi, sis," Krystal said. "What's going on? And who the heck was that sexy-sounding guy who answered the phone?"

Krystal. Molly had neglected to call and tell her own sister she was getting married. Now, she wondered if she had overlooked it because she hadn't wanted to tell Krystal she was marrying Garrett. Molly knew the best thing to do was get the telling over with, but there was no way she would tell Krystal the reasons behind the marriage.

"We've been having a wedding," she said, with forced gaiety.

"A wedding! Whose?"

"Mine."

"Yours!" Krystal squealed. "But we just spoke a couple of weeks ago, and you didn't say a word about getting married."

"I'm sorry. I guess I was still half asleep," Molly lied.

"Well, well, well," Krystal said with a laugh. "My baby sister married. Who's the lucky guy? Anyone I know?"

Molly took a deep breath and plunged. "As a matter of fact, you do. I just married Garrett Rambler."

"Garrett! Why, that sneaking lowlife! How dare he come back and sucker you into marrying him just so he could get his hands on the plantation again. How could you let him trick you like that, Molly?"

Molly was shocked at the venom in Krystal's voice. "He didn't trick me, Krys. I went into this of my own accord. And he didn't marry me to get the plantation. He was going to get it anyway."

"You lost the plantation?" Krystal said incredulously.

"I was about to."

There was silence on the other end of the line while Krystal digested this new information. Then she laughed, a knowing, unpleasant sound. "So you married Garrett so *you* could keep the plantation. Maybe I underestimated you, little sister. Maybe you're more like mother and me than I thought."

Krystal's sly allusion made Molly's actions sound cold and calculating... exactly like the type of thing Liz or Krystal would have done. The thought that she might be anything like either of them made Molly sick. She took little consolation in the knowledge that Krystal's accusation was only partly true. "I don't intend to discuss the reasons behind my marriage with you, Krys. Besides, you know I always cared for Garrett."

"That's right," Krystal cooed. "You did have a schoolgirl crush on him, didn't you." She laughed again. "Well, let me tell you, it'll take more than that to satisfy Garrett Rambler... if you know what I mean."

Molly's stomach lurched. She was afraid she did know what her sister meant. It sounded as though Krystal knew firsthand what it took to satisfy Garrett. The possibility left Molly feeling empty, a fact she hid out of pride.

"I think it's best we shelve this particular discussion, Krystal. What do you want?"

"I was going to see if you could lend me a little money, but I guess that's out of the question under the circumstances. You don't have any, and I doubt if your new husband would give me the time of day."

Molly didn't comment.

"Oh, well, I'll figure something out," Krystal said.

"You usually do."

Krystal laughed. "I'll talk to you soon, sis," she said. "You take care of that new husband."

"I will," Molly said through clenched teeth.

"Oh, and Molly," Krystal purred. "I understand exactly why Garrett fell for you. You're a beautiful woman. But a word of advice: don't ever forget that he's a Rambler."

Krystal hung up without explaining her comment. She didn't have to. She was reminding Molly that the Rambler men had uncontrollable appetites for beautiful women, and that just because Garrett was marrying her, didn't mean that he would change...or that she could hold him.

Molly clutched the receiver to her chest. She'd already thought of that, and had successfully pushed the possibility from her mind.

"Molly?"

She looked up. Garrett stood in the doorway, and Cindy, flushed with adoration, hung onto his arm. He looked dark and powerful and angry. A new, fresh rush of panic assaulted her. Dear God, what had she gotten into?

"Are you all right?" he asked.

Molly met his gaze unflinchingly. "I'm fine."

Garrett removed Cindy's hand from his arm and turned her toward the hallway, whispering something Molly couldn't hear. She watched her sister disappear. Garrett came closer, his sapphire eyes gemstone hard.

"What did that bitch say to you?"

Molly flinched at the fury in his voice. "Nothing."

"You're lying." He reached toward her. She gasped and took a step backward, but, surprisingly, Garrett didn't touch her. Instead, his hand closed around the telephone receiver that Molly wasn't even aware she was still holding.

Her shaking hands came up to cover her mouth. What had she done? Did she really think she could satisfy Garrett when other women—worldly women such as Krystal—couldn't?

He recradled the receiver, and his hard hands cupped her shoulders. "You're trembling," he said. "What did she tell you about me?"

Not wanting him to know how much Krystal's comments had upset her, Molly struggled to regain the nonchalance she'd contrived ever since Garrett had come back into her life. She lifted her steady gaze to his. "She said that you were a sneaking lowlife."

He shrugged. "You had already formed that opinion of me. What else?"

"That you wouldn't be satisfied with a schoolgirl crush."

He frowned. "What the hell does that mean?"

Molly lifted her chin. "It means that, like Cindy, I once had a crush on you."

There was no disguising the surprise in Garrett's eyes. "You? I didn't realize—"

She couldn't believe he hadn't known. "Never fear, Garrett," she interrupted, her voice dripping sarcasm, "I got over it."

"Molly?"

The sound of Ian's voice halted whatever answer Garrett might have made. Molly met her father at the door. Ian looked from Molly to Garrett and back again.

"Is everything all right?" he asked.

Molly forced herself to smile. "Everything is fine, Daddy," she assured him. "That was Krystal."

As she'd known it would, the fact that Krystal was the caller explained any tension he might feel in the room. "Oh. Well, everyone is waiting for you to finish opening gifts, and we were afraid something was wrong."

Molly urged a smile to her lips. "Tell them we'll be there in a second."

Ian cast another look at Garrett who was standing across the room. Once again, Molly and her new husband were alone.

"What else?"

Garrett asked the question as though they hadn't been interrupted. Molly was suddenly very tired. It was all too much. "She said for me not to forget that you were a Rambler."

There was no humor in his smile. "Excellent advice. But maybe she ought to remember that it works two ways."

"What do you mean?"

"You're Liz's daughter. Maybe I shouldn't forget that, either."

Even though it was a short drive to the Waverly, there was plenty of time for Molly to work herself into a state of anxiety. She'd seen the worry on her father's face as they pulled out of the drive amid a shower of birdseed. It was a worry she shared as the silence between her and Garrett stretched longer and longer. She wished he'd say something—anything— but he kept his eyes focused on the highway ahead, while his capable hands maneuvered the BMW through the gathering twilight.

Those same hands would soon be touching her, she realized, her panic escalating. She'd been worried enough about her wedding night, but now that Krystal's comments had whipped up Garrett's anger and her insecurities, she dreaded the night to come... dreaded the possibility that Garrett would be comparing her to Krystal. He was sensual, handsome, worldly and, like her mother and sister, had no doubt gained a great deal of sexual experience during his thirty-six years. She, on the other hand, could claim only one unsatisfactory, short-lived affair.

As he did in everything else, Garrett would expect nothing less than perfection in a lover, and she was far from that. The fact that she was so inhibited bothered her. He wanted her now, but what if she disappointed him? And what would happen to her when he tired of her? Molly leaned her head back and closed her eyes, plagued with worry and misery. She hadn't slept well for the past few weeks . . . months, actually. If only she could have a few moments' peace . . .

"Wake up."

The deep rumble of Garrett's voice intruded on Molly's brief respite from her problems. She didn't want to wake up. Sleep was a welcome escape. "Go 'way," she murmured.

"C'mon, *Petite*. We're at the hotel." The soft-spoken words were whispered half a second before she felt his lips nibbling her earlobe.

Reality surfaced with a vengeance. They were at the Waverly. They would soon be in the bridal suite that she herself had reserved for them. And if his actions were any indication, Garrett was more than ready.

Her eyes flew open. His face was close to hers, and the look in his eyes was one she was becoming familiar with. Desire. Hunger. A need so raw it left her breathless.

He reached out and fingered a curl that lay against her cheek, as if he liked the feel of it. "Has anyone ever told you you're sexy when you're asleep?"

Mesmerized by the look in his eyes, Molly could barely shake her head in response.

"You make all these sexy sounds." He lowered his head and rubbed the lock of hair against his lips, lips that were excitingly close.

Of its own volition, her head turned slightly until she could feel his mouth moving against her cheek when he spoke.

"You breathe fast, like your heart is racing," he said, his free hand moving to cover her left breast, covered by nothing but a flimsy satin teddy and a silk blouse.

Despite the uncertainty rising inside her, her breast swelled beneath his touch. His lips nuzzled the side of her neck, and his thumb rubbed against her nipple, kindling a sensation so intense that it threatened to drive her crazy. A noise, something between a sigh and a sob, escaped her partially open lips.

"And you make these funny little moans and groans," he said, as if the sound of her sigh cued his speech, "like someone is making slow, easy love to you."

He drew back to look at her, and Molly wondered if what she was feeling showed in her eyes.

"Did you know that?" he asked softly.

"No." The single word was a wisp of sound.

"I want to make slow, easy love to you."

"I know," she whispered.

"Let's go in."

There was no escaping the night. She knew that, had known it all along. All she could do was nod.

He drove the car beneath the canopy where a bellman offered to carry up the bit of luggage they needed
for their overnight stay. Garrett helped Molly from the
car and guided her up the marble steps, his hand resting casually against the small of her back.

They had just stepped through the revolving door
when a woman's voice shouted, "There they are!"

Molly glanced in the direction of the sound, and a
camera flashed, momentarily blinding her. Garrett
swore and pulled Molly against his side protectively.

"How in the hell did you find out where we were
staying?" he asked of an unseen person, while Molly
struggled to regain her vision.

A woman laughed. "I have a lot of relatives," was
the smug reply.

Mavis Davenport, Molly realized with a start. She
felt like crying. Why now, on top of Krystal's phone
call? Why wouldn't Mavis take no for an answer?

Pulling Molly along, Garrett stalked to the desk to
register and get the key. The bellman had disappeared. She wondered what the hotel personnel
thought of the scene Ms. Davenport was creating.

"So how was the wedding?" she asked Molly, instinctively choosing the path of least resistance.

"Wonderful," Garrett snapped just as the photographer captured his snarling face on film.

"And the bride wore...?" Mavis's voice trailed
away and she looked at Molly expectantly.

Key in hand, Garrett started across the lobby.
"Watch for the picture in Sunday's paper," he suggested. Held close to his side, Molly was almost run-

FIRST-CLASS ROMANCE

Mail This Heart TODAY!

And We'll Deliver:

**4 FREE BOOKS
A FREE GOLD-PLATED CHAIN
PLUS
A SURPRISE MYSTERY BONUS
TO YOUR DOOR!**

See Inside For More Details

SILHOUETTE DELIVERS FIRST-CLASS ROMANCE— DIRECT TO YOUR DOOR

Mail the Heart sticker on the postpaid order card today and you'll receive:

— 4 new Silhouette Special Edition® novels—FREE
— a lovely gold-plated chain—FREE
— and a surprise mystery bonus—FREE

But that's not all. You'll also get:

Convenient Home Delivery

When you subscribe to Silhouette Special Edition®, the excitement, romance and faraway adventures of these novels can be yours for previewing in the convenience of your own home. Every month we'll deliver 6 new books right to your door. If you decide to keep them, they'll be yours for only $2.74* each—that's 21¢ off the cover price plus only 69¢ postage and handling for the entire shipment!
There is no obligation to buy—you can cancel at any time simply by writing "cancel" on your statement or by returning a shipment of books to us at our cost.

Special Extras—FREE

Because our home subscribers are our most valued readers, we'll be sending you additional free gifts from time to time in your monthly book shipments as a token of our appreciation.

OPEN YOUR MAILBOX TO A WORLD OF LOVE AND ROMANCE EACH MONTH. JUST COMPLETE, DETACH AND MAIL YOUR FREE OFFER CARD TODAY!

FREE! gold-plated chain

You'll love your elegant 20k gold electroplated chain! The necklace is finely crafted with 160 double-soldered links and is electroplate finished in genuine 20k gold. And it's yours free as added thanks for giving our Reader Service a try!

Silhouette Special Edition®

FREE-OFFER CARD

4 FREE BOOKS

FREE GOLD-PLATED CHAIN

FREE MYSTERY BONUS

PLACE
HEART
STICKER
HERE

CONVENIENT HOME DELIVERY

MORE SURPRISES THROUGHOUT THE YEAR

☑ **YES!** Please send me four Silhouette Special Edition® novels, free, along with my free gold-plated chain and my free mystery gift as explained on the opposite page.

335 CIS 8165
(C-SIL-SE-08/90)

NAME _____

ADDRESS _____ APT. _____

CITY _____ PROVINCE _____

POSTAL CODE _____

Offer limited to one per household and not valid to current Silhouette Special Edition® subscribers. All orders subject to approval. Terms and prices subject to change without notice.

SILHOUETTE "NO RISK" GUARANTEE

There is no obligation to buy—the free books and gifts remain yours to keep. You receive books before they're available in stores. You may end your subscription anytime—just write "cancel" on your statement or return your shipment of books to us at our cost.

© 1990 HARLEQUIN ENTERPRISES LIMITED

MAIL THE POSTPAID CARD TODAY!

PRINTED IN U.S.A.

Remember! To receive your free books, gold-plated chain and mystery gift, return the postpaid card below. But don't delay!

DETACH AND MAIL CARD TODAY!

If offer card is missing, write to:
Silhouette Books, P.O. Box 609, Fort Erie, Ontario L2A 5X3

Business Reply Mail

No Postage Stamp Necessary if Mailed in Canada

Postage will be paid by

Silhouette Books ®
P.O. Box 609
Fort Erie, Ontario
L2A 9Z9

MAIL THE POSTPAID CARD TODAY!

ning to keep up with his ground-eating strides. It gave her some satisfaction to know that Mavis was having trouble teetering along in her spike heels.

Garrett reached the elevator and stabbed the button.

Undaunted, Mavis grabbed Molly's arm. "How'd you manage to snag him after what your mother did to Jon?"

Molly paled beneath the woman's malevolent, ice-blue gaze. Obviously Mavis didn't want news; she wanted sensationalism. Molly's legs threatened to give way, and her fingers tightened on Garrett's arm.

"Get your hands off her," he warned.

Mavis complied and, smiling a falsely benign smile, transferred her attention to him. "Aren't you afraid of history repeating itself?"

The muscle in Garrett's jaw tightened, but he only stared at the elevator doors and refused to answer.

"Weren't you and Molly's sister pretty thick back then? Didn't she dump you for some other guy? Some football player?" Mavis wheedled, determined to get some answers.

Surprised, Molly glanced up at his implacable features. Krystal had always maintained that Garrett was the one who'd done the cheating.

"Go to hell," Garrett said rudely as the elevator bell pinged and the doors slid open. He stepped inside, dragging Molly with him and pulling her into his arms. With her face pressed against his chest, she decided it was a nice place to be.

She sneaked a peek at the door and saw that Mavis had had the gall to step inside the elevator. "How does it feel to be married to a man your sister was once ... very close to?" she asked Molly, stressing the "very close."

"Get out."

With her eyes on the newswoman's face, Molly couldn't see Garrett's expression, but if his look was anything like his voice, *she'd* get out. A half second before the doors thudded shut, Mavis stepped out of the way, and Molly expelled a breath she wasn't even aware she'd been holding.

"The bitch," Garrett said, loosening his hold on Molly. "Are you okay?"

For the second time since he'd been back, Molly saw an emotion in his eyes that resembled tenderness. Or maybe it only seemed tender compared to the looks he'd given Mavis.

"I'm fine," she said with a nod.

The elevator stopped, and Garrett unlocked the door of the bridal suite, ushering her inside. Still in a state of shock from Mavis's attack, Molly was only marginally aware of her surroundings as he led her through the living area to the double doors that led into the bedroom.

"Wait here," Garrett said, pushing her gently into the room.

Surprised, Molly asked, "Where are you going?" She didn't want to be alone. She wanted him to hold her again.

"I'll wait out in the hall for the luggage, just in case those scavengers try to slip up here." His voice was as angry and uncompromising as the look in his eyes. "Then I'm going to find Mavis Davenport and kill that story—or her, whichever it takes."

Chapter Seven

Kill her?'' she repeated, her voice filled with horror and disbelief.

She was staring at him as if he were Jack the Ripper. Damn his temper, and damn Krystal and Mavis Davenport for ruining what was already a less-than-wonderful day. Molly looked as if she'd been run through an emotional wringer. Despite his fear that she was a carbon copy of the other women he'd dealt with, Garrett felt his fury become concern.

Fighting the unbidden softness, and the need to push back a strand of her dishevelled hair, he clasped the back of his neck. "It was a figure of speech," he said curtly, but her expression didn't change. He drew in a deep breath. "I'll get the luggage. You go take a warm bath."

Without a word, Molly turned toward the adjoining bathroom. She heard something that might have been a sigh before Garrett closed the doors and left her alone, facing the bed...a huge king-size, complete with a padded, white satin headboard and a mountain of lacy pillows.

The reality of the approaching night hit her without warning. It was one thing to worry about it, and quite another to be facing it. Drawing in a trembling breath, Molly went to the edge of the bed and sat down, trying to get some perspective on the day.

She was married. The ring on her finger proved that. Actually, it had gone better than she'd expected. Until Krystal called.

Don't think about Krystal. She was only trying to make you feel inferior, which is what she's tried to do all your life.

Rising restlessly, she went to run her bath. Garrett's telling her to take a bath had been an order, she thought as she dropped a generous dollop of expensive bath oil into the running water—not a suggestion. He was good at ordering people around.

Still, the way she was shaking inside, a bath might help relax her before he came to claim his conjugal rights. Molly's teeth clamped down on her bottom lip to stifle a giggle that bordered on hysteria.

Conjugal rights. Lord, she thought, stripping off her clothes. What a wedding night. The whole affair sounded like something straight from a nineteenth-century novel—including the wronged family and the gossipy biddy. Naked, she stepped into the warm water and slid down until the bubbles tickled her chin. Did other brides have former lovers and vicious journalists to contend with on their wedding days?

A sound in the bedroom made her tense for a moment, but when the bathroom door didn't open, she relaxed and let the steamy heat do its work. It was at least thirty minutes before she felt she was calm enough to face Garrett. Wrapping a towel around her slender body, Molly peeked into the bedroom and saw that he had placed her small suitcase on the bed. His belongings were scattered over the dresser and the door to the closet was ajar. Garrett himself was nowhere to be seen.

Fearful that he would come in before she was ready, Molly hurriedly donned the sheer white gown Shiloh had brought her. Remembering the feel of his hand on her breast, she wondered what Garrett would think of it. Heat seared her cheeks. Threading her fingers through the thick mane of her hair, she lifted it away from her neck.

Face it, Molly. You want him as much as he wants you. And if you weren't so afraid you'll disappoint him, you'd make the first move.

"So much for pride," Molly grumbled aloud. She felt better, though, for acknowledging her feelings.... It was one thing to admit to caring for Garrett and quite another to admit that his touch drove her crazy. She knew that he was only marrying her for the use of her body. Whatever came of this marriage, at least she could claim full control of his thoughts and attention when they made love.

She turned to pull back the sheets, but, catching sight of herself in the mirror, she stopped dead still.

Could the woman looking back at her be the same woman who had cowered in front of Mavis Davenport less than an hour ago? Fascinated, Molly stepped closer. This woman's hair had been taken down from the loose chignon she'd worn for the wedding. Uncombed, it cascaded halfway down her back in a riotous jumble of curls. Her eyes, enhanced by the skillful application of makeup, looked bigger than usual in the soft glow of the lamplight. The lace bodice of the gown had narrow ribbon straps and clung to her slender waist and the slight flare of her hips before swirling around her bare feet. Her nipples, rosy and swollen looking, were visible through the sheer lace, as was the dark triangle of hair at the juncture of her thighs. There was nothing—nothing!—left to the imagination, she realized wildly. On the heels of that thought came another: would Garrett like what he saw?

Whirling away from the mirror, she climbed into the big bed, pulled the lace and ribbon-trimmed sheet up to her chin and, her nerves tied into a hundred knots, waited.

And waited.

By ten o'clock, Garrett still hadn't come, and Molly had abandoned the idea that he was giving her time to accustom herself to the reality of the wedding night.

At eleven, wondering what on earth she would say to him, she gathered her courage in hand and peeked into the living room. It was empty. She went back to bed and wondered where he could have gone.

"A drink," she said out loud, as if by saying it forcefully enough she'd believe it. "He went downstairs to get a drink." She didn't dwell on the thought that Garrett wasn't the kind of man who would need a drink to fortify him before facing his bride.

By midnight, curiosity had given way to a strange combination of worry and vexation.

By one in the morning, vexation and worry succumbed to exhaustion, and Molly fell soundly asleep.

Barefoot, Garrett crossed the room at twenty past one. He sat on the edge of the bed and stared at Molly, drinking in the sight of her like a man gone too long without sustenance. She'd thrown back the tousled covers and the gown—what there was of it—had ridden up, revealing her shapely thighs and the sweet curve of her hip. Her breasts, more exposed than covered by the lace fabric of her gown, rose and fell with each breath that whispered through her parted lips. Dear God, she was more beautiful than he'd imagined.

His body responded predictably. He ached to strip off his clothes and take her, but knew he wouldn't. He'd been fighting the need to come back to the room and make love to her all evening. All that had guaranteed him any success were several hours of distance and several drinks. Now, even those methods threatened to fail him. He wanted her so much it was a gutdeep ache, but the call from Krystal played on his mind. That and the scene with Mavis Davenport.

Krystal's phone call had given him a much-needed reminder that there were things in his and Molly's past he shouldn't forget, no matter how strong her pull on his senses. The run-in with Mavis only reinforced that reminder.

Garrett's lips tightened. When he'd seen the look on Molly's face during Mavis's attack, he'd wanted to shake the newswoman until her teeth rattled. There had been real pain on Molly's face. Pain and what he could only speculate was fear. There was no way he was going to make love to her when she was obviously so distraught.

Even before that, he'd suspected that he couldn't make love to her. There was something too cold-blooded about sleeping with a woman who'd just as soon spit in your eye, even though the law gave you the right to do so.

Simply put, Molly had him tied in knots. He could have had her as his mistress, but no, he couldn't do that. He'd had to marry her. And, just as nothing less than marriage would do, he knew that nothing less than Molly's willing gift of her body would satisfy him. He knew he couldn't take her the way he had other women—without thought to anything but immediate gratification. What he didn't understand, was why he couldn't.

He damned himself for being a fool—after all, hadn't he married her to get her in the sack? Was he getting soft? Was it possible that he wasn't as bad as everyone thought he was? Hell, who knew? All he did know was that the woman lying before him was turning his life upside down.

Gently, so he wouldn't wake her, he grasped a handful of the red hair spilling across the white pillowcase like swirls of molten copper. It was soft to the touch. Soft, and curiously vibrant. He released her hair and placed his fingertip to the pulse beating in her bottom lip. Like her hair, her mouth was incredibly soft. She stirred, and he moved his finger away.

Touching her with feather-light strokes, he slid his hand from her knee to her hip, reveling in the satiny texture of her skin. His body, tormented by desire, throbbed. Dying to taste her mouth and the sweet promise of her breasts, Garrett rose, a silent curse on his lips.

Calling himself ten kinds of fool, he entered the bathroom. He stripped off his clothes, stepped beneath the stinging spray of a cold shower, and granted himself the release he refused to let himself find in the warmth of Molly's body.

Molly stretched, yawned and snuggled deeper beneath the single sheet covering her. She tucked her hands under her head, wincing when something sharp gouged her cheek and nudged her awake. Memory, like sunshine through the partially draped windows, seeped into her sleep-fogged mind.

It was a ring she felt beneath her cheek. Her wedding ring. She was married to Garrett, and last night had been her wedding night...a night she'd spent alone.

Her eyes flew open, and she turned her head cautiously. The other side of the bed was empty. It hadn't been slept in. Molly laid her head back down on the pillow. Why hadn't Garrett come to her, when he'd made it so obvious he wanted her? And more to the point, where was he? Tossing back the sheet, she eased her feet onto the pale-yellow carpet and reached for her robe.

What should she do now? Call someone to come and get her or try to find him? Either alternative would be embarrassing. She pulled on the robe and opened the doors to the living room. The sight that greeted her stopped her in her tracks. Clad in nothing but a pair of navy-blue bikini briefs, Garrett lay sprawled on the sofa, a heart-stopping vision of manhood personified.

Lured by his undeniable beauty, she crossed the room. He was tanned and fit, all supple muscle and taut skin...so much skin. His broad shoulders tapered down to a flat, muscle-ridged stomach, a stomach that, like his chest, was covered with an abundance of curly black hair that disappeared beneath the waistband of his shorts and dusted the length of his strong legs. Too long for the couch, one leg was draped over the arm, while the other was bent at the knee, his foot resting on the floor. The pose accentuated his stunning maleness.

Her hungry gaze traveled up over his chest to his face. Though his chin still had a determined look in repose, his usually unsmiling mouth looked softer in sleep. Lean, grooved cheeks showed a night's growth of beard that made him look even more exciting and dangerous.

Molly's hands clenched involuntarily. Her fingers itched to trace the curve of his upper lip, and she could almost feel the prickling of his whiskers against her palm. Needing to touch him as much as she needed her next breath, she lifted a hand to brush back the wayward lock of hair falling over his forehead.

Before she realized what was happening, Garrett reached out and caught her around the waist, jerking her down on top of him. Her body crashed into his, and a battalion of sensations stormed the fragile defenses she'd erected against the potency of his charm.

Afraid of what she would see on his face, she lifted her gaze. His eyes were closed, but there was an unmistakable intensity, a restrained anger in him as he slid his hands up the back of her legs. Palming her buttocks, he settled his body—his fully aroused body—between her parted thighs.

It felt so good Molly could have cried with pleasure. If she'd realized how wonderful it would feel, she might not have dreaded the night before so badly.

The night before. He hadn't come to her. Why? Instead of pressing herself closer, as she longed to do, she braced her hands on either side of his head and tried to wriggle free.

Grabbing her gown, Garrett dragged it up around her waist. His eyes opened slowly, almost lazily. They weren't cold now, she thought. They glowed with the same heat radiating from his body. His hands grasped her bare bottom and, holding her to him, he lifted his hips and rubbed the hardness of his body against her aching womanhood. "Be still," he growled, low in his throat. "Just be still."

With a whimper of longing, Molly dropped her head down and let Garrett have his way. He touched his lips to her hair; she turned her face so that her cheek rested against his. She could feel the perspiration dampening his skin and the increasing moistness gathering between her thighs with each erotic stroke of his body. Sensations she had only read about built inside her; she responded, pressing against him stroke for stroke, straining for a release that seemed so close.

Her arms began to tremble with her weight, but she was afraid that if she allowed any more of her body to touch him, she might not be able to stand it. When she felt his hands slide inside her robe to cup her breasts, Molly bit back a cry of need. She was still trying to accustom herself to the wild sensations flooding through her, when he lifted his head and pushed her breast upward, taking one tumescent nipple into his mouth. This time, she couldn't hold back the sound of pleasure that escaped her lips.

She felt his hands doing delicious, exciting things, felt his fingers against her... rubbing, caressing, driving her to the brink of a heady insanity before the heat of his manhood broached the dewy folds of her femininity. Molly relaxed and his hips surged upward. Burrowing his hand through the hair at the back of her head, Garrett fastened his mouth on hers, swallowing the sound of his name as it fell from her lips.

Buried deeply inside her, his mouth on hers, he began to move. Fast. Too fast. He didn't seem to be able to help himself. She was wet and hot, and he fit her so well...couldn't remember ever fitting a woman's body so well. Almost—the thought gave him momentary pause—as if he had been fashioned to fill her this way.

He'd wanted to take her slowly. Hell, he hadn't wanted to take her at all, not for a while...a long while, but the moment he'd felt her body against his, he knew he was lost. She was too beautiful, her body too tempting, his willpower too weak. He'd known she was trouble the minute he'd set eyes on her, but that hadn't stopped him from tying himself to her. From the very first, she'd messed up his thinking and made him break all his promises to himself.

Molly made him lose control...which gave him just one more thing to hold against her.

But not now. He held nothing against her now but his body and his lips that bruised the softness of hers in a series of kisses.

With a deft movement, without breaking the rhythm that bound them, he rolled over, putting her body beneath him. He felt her nails digging into the flesh of his hips. As impossible as it seemed, it was even better this way. So good he could hardly stand it. He looked at her. Her eyes were closed and her white teeth were buried in her bottom lip.

"Look at me," he commanded, his release a heartbeat away. He wanted to see what she was feeling when they climaxed. Needed to see if, like so many other things that could be faked, hers was real.

Molly opened her eyes. They were a cloudy, passion-glazed green that widened when he lifted her hips and gave a final, mind-shattering thrust. Wave after wave of intense pleasure surged through him, flinging him into a realm of sunshine and shattering him into tiny fragments of feeling....

When it was over, and the pieces of himself started falling back into place, a strange feeling of invincibility settled over Garrett. Yet, at the same time, he felt humbled by the experience...vulnerable, even. He didn't understand the conflicting emotions any more than he understood why he had denied himself her body the night before.

He tried to block out the sound of her ragged breathing that drove him slightly crazy, tried to ignore the softness of her breasts through the sheer fabric of her gown and the heady, flowery fragrance that emanated from her petal-soft skin. Impossible.

Maybe, he thought, trying to get some focus on his feelings, it was simply that if he'd tried to make love to her last night it would have seemed cold and calculating. Molly would have been expecting it—maybe even dreading it—and her capitulation would have been spurred by the knowledge that it was her duty. But this morning had caught them both with their defenses down. This morning was spontaneous, unplanned...and undeniably fantastic.

And because it was so fantastic, it was dangerous.

He couldn't allow himself the luxury of making love to her at his every whim. Sex could sometimes be too powerful. His judgment had been clouded by his need for a woman before, and the woman hadn't satisfied him nearly as completely as his new bride. It didn't matter that Molly had no idea of the power she held over him, or that he'd been younger and less in control of his feelings and actions back then. Molly Rambler was trouble. If he didn't watch out, she'd be calling the tune and he'd be dancing to it.

She drew a deep breath and moved restlessly beneath him. Thinking he was too heavy, he moved away and looked at her. She lifted damp, spiky lashes and stared back at him with tear-drenched eyes.

Garrett's heartbeats stumbled. Tears? Had he hurt her? She wasn't a virgin, but her body should have warned him that it had been a while for her. Dammit! He should have been easier with her, more careful.

Guilt and self-loathing drove the last trace of passion from his eyes and lent harshness to his voice. He sat up and adjusted his briefs. "Let's get out of here."

Still trying to come to terms with the emotions she'd experienced in his arms, Molly felt as if he'd slapped her. The disgust she read on his face and his curt words made the joy and hope she'd felt in the wake of his lovemaking seem naive, and the luminescent beauty they'd shared a few minutes before, paled to a sordid ugliness.

Humiliation overwhelmed her. Face flaming, she scrambled to her feet. Fighting the threat of tears, she started for the bedroom, drawing the cord of her robe around her as she went.

Garrett watched her go, regret filling his heart. How could he say he was sorry for making love to her, when he wasn't? Apologies were as foreign to him as the tenderness he felt sitting there watching her rigid, retreating back.

"Molly."

His voice stopped her. Chin high, she turned.

"I . . ." He paused.

"Regrets, Garrett?" she challenged in a cool, controlled voice that belied the hurt he thought he'd seen in her eyes.

His own eyes narrowed in suspicion. There was no trace of the fragility and softness he'd seen on her face only seconds before. All he could see was cool belligerence in her eyes. How could she change so fast? Had the tears been an act, then? He—hell, all the Rambler men—were notorious for falling for them. But not him. Not ever again. He'd vowed not to be taken in again—not even by his wife.

"No," he said, unable to humble himself as long as there was any doubt in his mind that he needed to. "No regrets."

Molly and Garrett stayed clear of each other while they got ready to leave the hotel, and they drove back to the plantation without saying a word except a necessary few. Garrett cursed himself for giving in to the feelings Molly generated in him, and Molly stared out the window without seeing the passing scenery, fighting the tears that burned beneath her eyelids.

As she'd feared, she had done something to displease him. Or maybe, she thought, her mind racing, it was something she should have done, and hadn't. In her naiveté, she'd let him make love to her, instead of doing her part to make certain that he received pleasure, too. Garrett was worldly, experienced. He was used to women who knew all the ways to please a man, women who had no qualms about using them.

She closed her eyes, allowing memories of the morning to wash over her. Her stomach tightened in response. Garrett's possession of her had been everything she'd dreamed it would be. Everything a woman could want. Recalling his cry of pleasure as he'd driven himself into her, she suddenly realized that no matter what he'd said or how he'd acted, he'd found his own satisfaction. And if that was true, what had triggered his anger?

Weary, miserable, her mind whirling with thoughts, Molly was wondering where she and Garrett went from there, when a terrifying thought struck her. They had made love without any protection. Logic told her that the chances of her getting pregnant from one encounter was slim, yet the thought of having Garrett's child was both thrilling and frightening. What kind of father would he make? Would he have Ian's gentleness and understanding during his wife's bouts of morning sickness and the awkwardness of pregnancy? Or Jon's patience in steeping his child with a sense of his past?

The reality of the uncompromising look on Garrett's face when he'd told her he'd never let her go if

she had his child, sent a shiver of apprehension dancing down her spine.

She clenched her teeth. Getting pregnant was
something she couldn't afford to do. Not until she was
a bit more confident that she and Garrett had come to
some sort of an understanding. Which meant that,
until that day came—like it or not—she had to find the
strength to say no.

Chapter Eight

June aged to a fine, golden dryness.

True to his word, Garrett killed whatever story Mavis Davenport had planned to write. The only thing in the Sunday paper was a picture of Molly that Ian had taken and a brief write-up Veronica had sent in. Molly didn't know if Garrett had threatened Mavis, or if he'd paid her off, and she didn't care, as long as the woman left them alone.

To her surprise, fighting off Garrett's attention was the last thing she needed to worry about. Remembering the morning they'd spent, she knew that her vow to say no to him was wasted energy, so she'd gone to town and equipped herself with over-the-counter birth control. Not that she'd needed it. Garrett hardly talked to her—much less made a pass—and when he did speak, it was to ask her something about the plantation. Though they lived in the same house, they maintained separate bedrooms. In fact, she began to worry that he'd never make love to her again.

To any observers, they appeared to be the perfect newlywed couple. Molly fixed breakfast, which they usually shared on the screened-in porch off the kitchen—Garrett reading the paper, Molly doing the crossword puzzle. Garrett spent his days outside, fixing fences, repairing the barn...doing whatever things men did when they had two hundred acres to care for. Molly worked in her garden, canning and freezing vegetables as they ripened, cleaning the house and doing the tours and dinners as usual. Garrett would come in for a light lunch and wouldn't return until dark for his dinner, which made Molly late getting out of the kitchen. She didn't say anything about the inconvenience. It helped pass the hours from dinner till bedtime.

After they ate, Garrett usually went into his study to mull over the books and read the stacks of literature he'd received from the Department of Agriculture on crawfish farming. Molly would watch TV and think how little her life had changed since she married. Other than cooking more than usual and having more laundry, Garrett's presence in the house had hardly upset the rhythm of her days. Generally, it was life as usual, except that she didn't have to worry about paying the bills. Actually she was more lonely with Garrett in the next room than she had been living in the house by herself.

By the end of June, she'd had enough. The heat and lack of rain made her feel as listless and wilted as the flowers sunning outside the windows. She was cranky and out of sorts, and she'd reached the point where she was spoiling for a good old-fashioned fight. At least if they were fighting, she'd know that she had Garrett's undivided attention.

On the day Molly finally decided to corner him and demand that they do something about their living arrangements, Garrett yanked the rug out from under her by telling her he was going on a trip for a couple of days . . . alone.

"Did it ever occur to you to tell me you were going?" she stormed, furious at his cavalier attitude.

Garrett frowned. "I am telling you."

"I mean, before you're literally walking out the door," she explained with exaggerated patience. "Did you ever think of asking me if you could go?"

"Ask you?" His voice was deadly quiet and filled with disbelief. "I haven't *asked* if I could go somewhere since I was sixteen years old. And I'm sure not gonna start now."

"Did you ever think of talking it over with me . . . asking if I minded your going?" she persisted.

"No. Why should I?"

"Because I'm your wife."

Garrett didn't mask his surprise. He raked a hand through his unruly dark hair. "And that gives you the right to know my every move?"

"This isn't your every move. I never ask what you're doing through the day. But this is an overnight trip."

"So?"

"So, you should have told me you were going. Do you mean you never told Lacey when you were going to be away?"

"Never."

"Maybe you should have," she said boldly, bluntly, throwing caution to the wind.

"Meaning?"

She wanted to tell him that she was tired of spending so much time by herself when he was sitting in the next room and she was tired of eating while he stuck his nose in the paper. But pride forbade her.

"Meaning that maybe if you'd shared a little more of yourself, confided a little more about how you felt, what was going on in your life, things might have been different between the two of you."

For long moments they stood there, looking at each other, weighing the situation and waiting.

"I'm going to North Louisiana," Garrett said at last, volunteering the information she wanted.

Molly expelled the breath she'd been holding. A breakthrough! Minor, but a breakthrough. "Do you mind my asking where in North Louisiana?"

"Bossier City. Louisiana Downs, to be exact. The Pick Six is the biggest it's been all year," he told her, as if that should be reason enough for his going.

"And you're going to gamble on winning it?" she said, her heart sinking.

"Don't worry," he said, with a sardonic twist of his lips, "I'm not going to gamble away the plantation."

"Very funny, Garrett," she snapped. "You act as if the plantation is the only thing I care about."

"Isn't it?" he countered.

She shifted her weight to one foot and crossed her arms in front of her. "Not that it matters to you, but since this is likely going to be the only marriage I'm ever a part of, I care about what happens to it."

Garrett saw the familiar lift of her chin and the spark of fire in her green eyes. Lord, she was gorgeous when she was riled. The familiar excitement curled inside him. He'd deliberately stayed away from her, working until he was exhausted or it was dark—whichever came first—spending the hours from supper until bedtime pacing the floor of his study. Hell, he even tried to avoid looking at her, because every time he did, he felt the desire rise up. As it was doing now.

It occurred to him, and not for the first time, that he liked it when she was angry. It occurred to him, too, that maybe she was right. Maybe things between them would be better if he shared more of his thoughts and plans with her. He intended for this to be his last marriage, too. Hadn't he married Molly because she shared his passion for the past and cared as much about the plantation's future as he did?

Passion. That's what they shared. Passion. And not just for the plantation. Maybe, he thought, eyeing her slender body, he was making a mistake by denying himself the thing he wanted the most. After all, if he recognized the dangers involved in making love to her, he could be on the watch for them.

Molly was unhappy with the way things were between them. Her short speech had told him that. So was he. He hadn't meant to make her angry by not telling her he was going out of town, and he hadn't realized that talking things over with her meant so much, but he wasn't used to checking in with anyone.

He looked at her, sincerity in his blue eyes. He didn't want this marriage to go down the drain, either...whatever the reason. "Believe me, *Petite*," he said, "our marriage matters to me. It matters to me very much."

It was one of the longest weekends Molly had ever lived through. She prayed Garrett would lose his money and learn a lesson. She prayed he wouldn't lose, so that he would have the money to put in his crawfish farm and not have to put up the paintings as collateral.

And, by Sunday night, she'd convinced herself that Garrett meant it when he said the marriage meant a great deal to him, too. Of course, she reminded herself, she was good at make-believe, always had been. It also was easy to convince herself that the look in Garrett's eyes when he left had been desire.

It was almost dark on Sunday when she heard a loud engine and a clattering sound out front. Rushing to the window, she saw a dusty pickup and stock trailer heading for the barn. Who on earth? she wondered, going to the door.

Barefoot, she ran down the steps and across the yard. As she reached the gate, a lanky man wearing a sweat-stained straw Stetson got out of the truck.

"Can I help you?" Molly called as he started for the rear of the trailer.

"No thanks," the man said, "I can handle it." He spit a stream of tobacco juice that pocked the soft dust of the driveway. Without another word, he went to the back of the trailer and started unfastening the door.

"What are you doing?"

The stranger turned and looked at her as if she was crazy, then cocked his hat to the back of his head. "Well, ma'am," he said patiently, "I'm unhooking this here gate, so's I kin unload these here horses."

"Horses!" Molly cried. "I'm sorry, but you've made a mistake. I wasn't expecting any horses."

The man shrugged and nodded his head toward the highway. "Jist hang on a minute."

Looking in the direction of the highway, Molly saw Garrett's BMW pull into the lane. Thank goodness! Maybe he could help get this mess straightened out. Wearing tight Levi's and a smile, Garrett got out of the car and started toward them, his boots making little dust clouds with every step he took.

The genuineness of the smile and the shock of seeing it caught Molly off guard.

"Hi," he said, bending and brushing her mouth with a light, unexpected kiss. "How was your weekend?"

"F-fine," she said, stunned by his behavior and swamped by the exotic masculine scent of his co-

logne. He released her and approached the trailer. She
jogged a few steps to catch up with him. "Garrett, this
man thinks he's supposed to unload some horses
here."

"He is."

"What?" For the second time in the span of a minute Molly was shocked.

"I didn't win the Pick Six, but I did hit a couple of
big exactas," he told her. "I found a guy in Minden
who had a couple of quarter horses to sell, and I remembered that you used to love to ride. And, since
there have always been horses at Rambler's Rest, I
decided to buy one for each of us."

The smile was back, she noticed with a racing heart.
An honest-to-goodness smile. Molly couldn't resist the
pull of it on her heartstrings. If she couldn't resist him
at his worst, how could she at his best?

She couldn't believe he remembered that she loved
horses. Actually, it had been Garrett who taught her
to ride. She could still recall his patience as he'd shown
her how to sit, how to hold the reins, how to put the
horse through its paces. The sweet memory of his
smile and the pride she'd felt at his praise brought a
sudden sting of tears to her eyes.

"Come see," he urged.

Molly had no choice but to go. Stepping onto the
running board of the trailer, she looked through the
metal slats and saw two stocky horses—one a chest-
nut mare, the other a buckskin gelding. They were
sleek and dappled and, if anything, a bit too fat. They

were beautiful animals, and she was touched by his thoughtfulness.

"Well," he asked, "what do you think?"

Molly turned and looked up at him. There was expectancy in his eyes, and a gleam that told her he was pleased with his purchases. Again, she felt that tug on her heartstrings. What she thought was that he was wonderful and she loved him. But all she said was, "They're beautiful, Garrett. Thank you."

They spent the next two hours getting the horses settled. Garrett had already made the necessary repairs to the barn. He had replaced rotted boards and nailed back loose ones wherever necessary. The mow had been swept free of old straw and hay, and the tack room, too, was clean and boasted new shelving.

They worked side by side, Garrett wetting down the stalls and filling them ankle deep with fresh straw while Molly scrubbed out the feed and water buckets and hung sweet-smelling alfalfa in mesh bags.

Though it was near dusk, it was still hot. Feeling zapped by the heat, Molly blotted her sweating face on her shoulder and wished she was inside under a fan...or better yet, in her bedroom, one of the few rooms in the house that was air-conditioned. She couldn't remember a summer the heat had bothered her the way it had this year. Turning on the water hose, she twisted the nozzle until it gave out a fine mist. She directed the spray to her face, and the cold water took her breath away.

"What are you doing?"

Molly jumped and whirled toward the sound of Garrett's voice, inadvertently aiming the hose at him. She watched in horror as water hit him in the face and chest. Garrett's mouth dropped open in shock and he threw up his arms, as if such a puny defense would save him from further drenching.

Pointing the nozzle toward the ground, Molly faced him, fearing the worst. Rivulets of water trickled from his hair and down his lean cheeks. Oh, his face! The look on his ruggedly handsome face was so comical that her fear evaporated. She bit back the giggle rising in her throat, but to no avail.

Garrett swiped his hair back and brushed at a drop of water clinging to the end of his nose. "It isn't funny."

"Yes, it is," she said, smiling.

Without warning, Garrett pounced, grabbing her free hand and grabbing the hose from the other. Holding her at arm's length, he turned the nozzle toward her. Molly shrieked and tried to pull away, but a laughing Garrett held her in his grip. Trying to tug her hand free, she thrashed her head from side to side to avoid the water.

"Gar-rett!" she wailed. She faced him bravely, her free hand planted on her hip, while the cloud of spray rained down upon her.

"What?" he asked, innocently aiming the water at the ground.

"This isn't funny." She tried to look stern, but with a smile twitching at the corners of her mouth, she failed miserably. This was the Garrett she'd learned to love, and Molly gave herself over to the happiness welling up inside her.

He grinned and relaxed his hold on her wrist. "Yes, it is," he said, mimicking her earlier comment.

"Beast!" she quipped and, with a deft motion, freed her hand. Pivoting on her sneaker-clad feet, she made a bid for freedom. Garrett lunged for her, hooking his fingers in the belt loop of her jeans. Molly slipped in the mud and, with another screech, fell to her knees. Her weight along with the suddenness of her fall pulled Garrett off balance, and he landed on top of her. Only a quick movement of her head saved her from getting a mouth full of dirt.

Struggling against a sudden dizziness, Molly struggled to fill her lungs with the oxygen that Garrett's weight had knocked from them. She felt him roll away, felt his hands on her shoulders as he turned her over and forced her to sit up.

"Are you okay?" he asked, pulling her to her feet.

She nodded and pushed a strand of hair back with a grubby hand, leaving a smear of mud across her forehead. "Just a little winded."

"I could have crushed you."

Was it just wishful thinking, or did she hear a note of concern in his voice? "I'm fine." She glanced down at the hose which was still spraying water...all over their feet. "Maybe you'd better turn off the water."

He shut off the spray and looped the rubber hose into a neat pile. Then he looked at Molly standing there, her hair plastered to her shapely head, her cotton blouse clinging damply to her bare breasts...

breasts with nipples gone pebble hard from the chill of the water. "What were you doing?" he asked again, dragging his gaze from the tempting globes to her face.

"Trying to cool off."

He looked at her wet clothes and smiled again, stealing a bit more of Molly's heart. "And did it work?"

She thought of the heat pulsating through her and shook her head. Then, realizing that her answer was a dead giveaway, she blurted, "I mean, yes. I'm cooler."

"And muddier." His look seemed to say that he knew what she was really feeling.

Awkwardness, worthy of Molly's gauche teenage years, filled her. She'd wanted his attention, and now that she had it, she didn't know what to say. Before she could come up with a suitable comeback, he glanced at the horses munching contentedly on their hay and said, "We're finished here. Let's go in and get cleaned up."

Strangely elated, Molly nodded and followed him out of the barn into the gathering twilight, wondering if her eagerness showed. With a feeling of undeniable anticipation building inside her, she remembered his kiss of welcome and the readiness of his smile. Maybe he'd loosen up a little more now. Maybe this was a turning point in their relationship.

Then, again, maybe it wasn't, Molly thought, four hours later as she tossed in her bed. Maybe her relationship with Garrett was doomed to be one-side.

Which was a pity, considering that her feelings were growing stronger each day.

She flipped over onto her back and glanced at the red numbers on her clock. Nearly eleven p.m. Eleven p.m. and she was still awake. Normally, she was asleep before the ten o'clock news was over. It was unbearably hot outside. *She* was hot...and not all of the heat tormenting her was caused by the weather.

Arching her back, she unfastened the tiny buttons marching primly down the front of her sleeveless, scoop-necked cotton gown and pulled the opening wider, exposing more of her breasts to the languid breeze that shuffled through the screened doors of her room. Outside, on the front gallery, Silvie's bells tinkled softly.

Molly thought about getting up and turning on the air conditioner, but she was used to doing without it to save on her electric bill. And just because Garrett was now responsible for that bill, didn't mean she was going to take advantage of that fact.

What was Garrett doing, anyway? she wondered, flipping her pillow over to the cool side. Was he running his window unit and sleeping away the hot summer night? For the hundredth time, she replayed the moment his mouth met hers in that unexpected kiss of greeting and the warmth and softness in his voice when he'd said his simple hello.

She smiled in the darkness. She couldn't believe he'd actually played in the water with her. That wasn't in character for the new Garrett Rambler at all. She wondered what had happened in Bossier City to change his attitude. She wondered if the change was permanent or just a momentary lapse.

A recollection of the kiss made her wonder why he hadn't come to her since that first morning. Memory of that morning sent a throbbing awareness tingling through her. Her breasts ached for his touch, and, to ease the pain, she pressed against them with her hands. They felt tender and swollen...the way they'd felt after Garrett had made love to her.

Stop it, Molly!

Angry with herself for her wanton feelings, she got up and went to the doors that led to the gallery. Wisps of cloud were draped across the silver sliver of moon, and night sounds wafted through the air. Molly felt an inexorable peace steal through her. Going to the railing, she lifted her hair from the back of her neck, letting the faint breeze cool her heated flesh.

After several seconds, she felt the back of her neck prickle, as if someone was staring at her. Whirling abruptly, she saw Garrett leaning against a far pillar, smoking and watching her. She suppressed a cry of surprise and grasped the railing for support.

He wore only unbuttoned, faded jeans that accentuated his manhood in a breathtaking way. His hair, still shower wet, was combed back from his face. The severity of the style threw the strong lines of his face into stark relief against the blackness of the night and warned her anew that he could be a dangerous adversary.

"Can't you sleep, either?" he asked, his voice a husky rumble. He pushed away from the pillar and sauntered barefoot across the porch toward her.

Molly shook her head and tried to keep her eyes focused on his face, not on his bare chest or on the fact that he might not be wearing anything beneath the skin-tight jeans. "I was too hot."

"Me, too."

The comment was innocent enough, but the look in Garrett's eyes as they trailed from her face down over her chest told her that he was talking about something entirely different.

Molly fought the urge to reach up and close the gaping bodice of her gown. What good would it do? The fine lawn fabric was so sheer he could see through it anyway. In a moment's honesty, she admitted that she wanted him looking at her with that hungry expression in his eyes. She wanted more than the vague wish for her marriage to "work."

What she wanted was Garrett. Now. That minute. And for the rest of her life. Somehow, she had to figure out how to win him...not just for a night, but forever.

You can start with a night, Molly. The reminder came out of nowhere, a gentle thought with no beginning, no end.

Yes, she could, she thought, as a feeling of power stirred inside her. For once, she'd play the game his way. She was ready. There would be no shyness, no hesitation, no acts of innocence. She'd be the woman he wanted...at least for one night, and maybe...just maybe, if she was woman enough, one night would lead to another...and another. It was worth the gamble, she thought. After all, she was a Rambler now, and all Ramblers gambled now and then.

Gathering her courage, she shook her hair back and looked up at him. "I thought it would be cooler out here. I was wrong. It's hotter."

Garrett took a deep drag from the cigarette and blew the smoke skyward, his eyes never leaving hers. "Yeah. I believe it is."

Molly reached up and brushed a strand of hair away from her face, a gesture that bared the swell of her breast to the pouting nipple. "Any ideas?" she asked provocatively.

"I've already tried a cold shower. It didn't help."

"Mmm," she said with a nod. "The fan doesn't help much, either." She turned to look over the moon-shadowed lawn. "Not in any way that counts."

"I know what you mean." Garrett flipped the cigarette out across the dew-wet grass and leaned his hip against the railing. "There's always the hair of the dog, so to speak."

Without warning, he slid his arm around her waist and pulled her against him, thigh to thigh. Startled by the sudden action, Molly was quiet in his embrace. She could feel the strength of his arms and the hardness of his body blossoming against hers. Garrett's eyes blazed in the darkness. "What do you mean?" she whispered.

He laid his hand against her cheek, his thumb grazing the fullness of her bottom lip. "Sometimes," he said, "when you have a hangover, another drink makes it better." He lowered his head until the sweetness of his breath caressed her face. "So I wonder if, after you've made love with someone and you still want them so much you hurt, a kiss will stop the pain."

Before Molly could answer, his mouth touched hers in a kiss so light it might only have been the promise of a kiss. Her lips parted, and she felt his hold on her face tighten in response. He slanted his mouth across hers, kissing her hotly, sweetly. He tasted of mouthwash and tobacco and man, and Molly couldn't get enough. Pressing herself closer to him, she slid her arms around his back, reveling in the supple play of skin and muscle beneath her hands.

He released his hold on her face, and she felt the soft whisper of his fingertips down her neck. Forsaking her mouth, his lips followed the course of his fingers, stringing a trail of kisses downward. His tongue made a darting foray into the hollow at the base of her throat, and his palm flattened, fingers spread, against her breastbone.

He lifted his head and looked at her, his eyes glittering dangerously. "It didn't work," he told her in a desire-laden voice. "I'm hotter than ever."

"I know." Her voice was the merest thread of sound.

"I'll make you a bet," he said. "I'll bet I can put out the fire . . . at least for a while."

She knew exactly what he was talking about. She wanted him to quench the flame blazing inside her, even though she knew it was a temporary measure at best. In reply, Molly leaned forward and touched her lips to one bronze nipple, circling the hard nub with her tongue.

Garrett's breath hissed out through clenched teeth. Pushing her away, he went to the chaise longue and pulled the padded cushion onto the floor. Then he took Molly's hand, urging her to join him. She acquiesced without a word, going into his arms and lowering her lips to his in a thorough kiss. Taking the neckline of her partially unbuttoned gown, he spread it wide and dragged it downward, lifting and nudging her breasts free, baring her quivering flesh to his gaze.

The thought of his mouth touching her made her heart race. And the heat in his eyes was nothing compared to the fire blazing hotter and higher inside her.

He reached out and skimmed a knuckle over the ripe fullness of her breast, letting his fingers slide down the upper slope and circling her nipple with a light touch. Molly closed her eyes and gave herself over to the feelings burning inside her. Garrett took her breasts in his hands and, plumping the soft globes upward, he brushed his thumbs over the tight, tumescent tips.

He lowered his head, and his mouth caressed her breasts. Molly responded by plowing her fingers through his hair and tightly holding him close. Garrett kissed first one breast and then the other, his tongue bathing her with moisture and fanning the glowing embers of her desire. If his kisses made her wild, the touch of his mouth against her breasts drove her crazy. Each tug of his lips increased the pleasurable throbbing in her lower body.

The wind chimes danced in the sudden breath of air that gusted off the bayou. It whispered that she and Garrett belonged to the night, as she would soon belong to him. Soon . . . soon now, she would recapture the heady fulfillment of his possession.

The sound of an approaching car pierced the sweetness of the moment and shattered Molly's pretense that she and Garrett were the only two people in the word. Like a teenager caught necking in a car, panic rushed through her. Pushing herself to her elbows she looked toward the highway. Twin headlights sliced through the black of the night as a car pulled into the circle driveway. Wonderful. Someone was coming, and here she was making out with her husband on the gallery. She tried to sit up, feeling more than a little sorrow for the lost moment.

"What is it?" Garrett's voice sounded slow and deep, as if he were speaking from the bottom of a deep well.

"Someone's coming."

"Damn!" The single word was resonant with frustration. Garrett rolled away from her and peered through the slats of the railing. When he saw the car, he lowered himself to his back and threw his forearm over his face. "It's a cab," he said. "Who is it?"

Molly glanced at the car. He was right. Her own thwarted desire caused her irritation level to rise. "How would I know? I wasn't expecting anyone."

The cab pulled to a stop, and the driver got out, heading for the trunk.

"Sorry," Garrett apologized. "You'll have to get the door. I'll be right behind you, but I'm not in any shape to welcome guests...or strangers, either, for that matter."

Molly was busy trying to match buttons to tiny button holes. "What?"

"Let's say I'm visibly aroused, *Petite*," he said.

Shocked by the bluntness of his statement, Molly flung her hand over his mouth. "Shh. They'll hear you."

Garrett pulled her down on top of him and gave her a lingering kiss while the door of the cab slammed shut. "Who cares?" he asked in her ear. "They shoulda called first."

"Maybe so, but they didn't," Molly said, as the sound of voices— one masculine, one feminine—filtered upward. "It's a woman. Do you think it's Shiloh?"

"No."

"You don't think something's happened, do you?" she whispered. "Something with Dad?"

"Veronica would have called."

"You're right. Come on, Garrett. Let me up."

He released her with a sigh and, rising, helped her to her feet. The sound of the brass knocker being pounded against the oak door, echoed in the stillness of the night.

"Be real quiet tiptoeing inside," he whispered in her ear. "Then you can act like whoever it is woke you up."

Which was exactly what she was going to do. Molly eased back inside and crossed to the door of her room, grabbing a robe on the way. A quick glance over her shoulder told her that Garrett was following close behind. Getting into the robe and turning on lights as she went, Molly descended the stairs to the front door.

A glance through the leaded window panes on either side of the door revealed nothing but the shadowy figure of a woman facing the road. Knowing Garrett was nearby, Molly flicked back the night bolt and turned the knob.

The woman pivoted slowly, a smile on her very familiar face.

"Hello, Molly."

Chapter Nine

Krystal!''

Krystal gave her a perfunctory hug, and Molly was enveloped for a moment in the heady scent of Opium. She couldn't have been more shocked if Liz's ghost stood on the porch. Maintaining that she loathed the plantation—which was why Molly got it and Krystal got Liz's jewels and cash—Krystal hadn't set foot on the place since their mother's funeral.

Krystal stepped aside, and Molly's gaze veered anxiously from her sister's perfectly made up face to the four large suitcases sitting on the porch. "What are you doing here?"

"I've left Freddy," Krystal said, as if that were explanation enough. Stepping back, she picked up a garment bag and an eel-skin overnight case. "I'm broke. I had no place to go, so I thought of you." She looked at Molly with pain-filled eyes. "You don't mind, do you?"

Mind? Molly wanted to scream. Of course she minded. There was no way she could stand having Garrett and Krystal in the same house together when she suspected that they'd once been lovers.

While Molly stood there wondering how she could get rid of her sister, Krystal pushed past her into the wide hallway. She'd gone no more than half a dozen steps when she saw Garrett lounging against the newel post, his arms crossed over his bare chest, a half smile on his lips. She stopped in her tracks.

"Well, if it isn't the bridegroom in all his glory." She glanced back at Molly, who stood watching with a thoughtful look on her face, and then allowed her insolent gaze to rove from Garrett's bare feet up to his tousled head. In a studied gesture, she straightened her shoulders, an act that drew attention to her perfectly shaped breasts. "I hope I didn't interrupt anything."

Embarrassed that Krystal may be imagining that she and Garrett had been making love, Molly cast him a worried look. "As a matter of fact, you did," he said.

For just an instant, Molly thought her sister looked nonplussed. If so, she recovered quickly and flung him a brittle smile. "Ah, well, the night is young. I'll get settled in and leave you lovebirds alone. Don't give me a second thought."

Right, Molly thought in disgust, as if she and Garrett could pick up where they left off...knowing Krystal was in the next room.

"We won't," Garrett said, surprising them both.

Suspicion lurked in Krystal's eyes as she turned to Molly. "I suppose it's all right to use my old room."

What could she say? Molly wondered. Sorry, sister dear, but I don't want you within a continent of my husband?

"Garrett, be a dear and take my bags up, will you?" Krystal ordered, not waiting for an answer. She shrugged out of her suit jacket and headed for the parlor. "I'm dying for a drink and a hot bath."

Krystal hadn't even waited for her answer, Molly thought. "I'm sorry, Krys," she said, glad something wasn't going Krystal's way, "but I'm all out of liquor."

"What do you have, then? I can't drink coffee. I'll be awake all night."

"I have a couple of beers in the fridge," Garrett offered, lunging away from the banister post.

"Beer?" From the tone of Krystal's voice, Garrett might have offered her arsenic.

"You used to like beer," he reminded her.

The hardness of Krystal's face softened at the thought of Garrett recalling her likes and dislikes. Smiling a smile full of wiles and witchery, she moved closer to him. "What else do you remember about me?"

Garrett's mouth twisted. "That you liked flashy cars and rich men."

Krystal's laughter was throaty and full-bodied. "That hasn't changed and neither have you." As though Molly wasn't there, Krystal reached out and placed her hand on Garrett's bare chest. "You're still sharp tongued and damned good-looking."

Molly couldn't stifle the sound of surprise that escaped from her throat.

Garrett flicked Molly a glance as his fingers closed around Krystal's wrist. "If that was a compliment, thank you. But you're wrong, Krystal. I've changed a lot." Before she could reply, he released her and stepped back. "If you want the beer, you know where the kitchen is."

"Yes, I do," she said, a frown marring the smoothness of her forehead.

"Molly."

She dragged her gaze from her sister's face. "What?"

"Is Krystal's room ready?"

"Yes, but . . ."

"Then why don't you go visit with her, and I'll get the luggage," he suggested.

"Sure," Molly said with commendable nonchalance. She didn't want to visit with her sister. She wanted to go back upstairs with Garrett and finish what they'd started on the gallery. Still, at least Garrett was taking his partially naked body out of Krystal's predatory sight.

"I'm going to turn in when I finish carrying the suitcases upstairs."

Molly's heart sank. It didn't sound as if Garrett had a night of lovemaking on his mind, after all. Of course, she had to agree that if anyone could put a damper on things, it was Krystal. "Fine," she told him, careful to keep her gaze averted.

"G'night, Garrett," Krystal purred. "I'll see you later."

Damn her! The way it sounded, Krystal was planning on rendezvousing with Garrett the minute she herself was asleep. Molly gave him a fulminating look and, turning, followed Krystal out of the room.

Krystal flipped on the kitchen light and plopped down in a chair, instead of getting her beer. Experience had taught Molly that Krystal expected to be waited on. Well, she might wait on her, but she wasn't going to be made a doormat. Not ever again, and especially not by Krystal. "What'll it be, Krys? Iced tea or the beer?"

"Oh, the beer, I suppose. At least it will help me relax." Krystal's curious gaze roamed the kitchen. "You've redone the place since Mama died."

Molly heard the underlying question behind the statement: how could Molly have updated the kitchen when money was supposed to be so tight?

"I had to renovate a bit when I decided to start doing the dinner parties," Molly explained and wondered why she felt she had to defend her actions.

Hoping to change the subject, she asked, "What happened with Freddy? Obviously you didn't convince him there was nothing going on between you and Spiro."

"Obviously," Krystal pouted.

Molly set the bottle of beer on the table. "What happened?"

Krystal's smile was saccharine sweet. "May I have a glass, please?"

Molly smiled back in kind. "Certainly."

Once the beer was poured into a glass and Molly got settled into the chair across from her sister, Krystal seemed ready to talk. "Remember I told you I wasn't going to sleep with Spiro right off the bat? Well, I didn't. But, you know, me, sis . . . I had to do it. If for no other reason than to find out if the old spark was there."

"And?" Molly prodded.

"Surprisingly, it wasn't."

Krystal took a sip of her beer and licked the foam from her upper lip with a delicate, feline gesture.

"What I did worm out of him was why he dumped me for Mama."

Molly's eyes widened in surprise. "He told you that?"

A wicked smile curved Krystal's luscious lips. "Get enough ouzo in Spiro and he'll tell you anything."

"I'll bet." Molly shook her head. Krystal was definitely in another league. "If the truth were known, I'll bet you slept with him more to find out about Mama than to see if the spark was still there."

"If the truth were known," Krystal admitted, "you're only partially right. You know what they say about a woman scorned. Well, I wanted to lead Spiro on and then dump him. Just so he'd know how it feels."

"And did you?"

Krystal gave a definite, satisfied nod. "Darn right. The only catch was that Freddy found out. He wasn't too pleased. It seems that to him fidelity ranks right up there with virginity." She laughed throatily. "Poor Freds. He didn't get either with me."

"Does he want a divorce?"

Krystal nodded, all smiles gone. She raised beseeching eyes to her sister. "I know we haven't been close, Molly, but you're the only family I have. I realize you and Garrett are still on your honeymoon, and I hate to interfere, but I didn't know where else to go. I was broke and desperate. I borrowed the money to come home from Freddy's sister."

Loving Garrett and having that love spurned made Molly sympathetic to her sister's plight. Maybe she really was in love with Freddy—as in love as someone like Krystal could be. And if she was, Molly understood her pain. She should know better than to believe any of Krystal's stories, but there was something in her voice that begged Molly to understand, and being Molly, she did.

Falling in love must have made me soft in the head. She sighed. "How long will you be staying?"

"I don't know. Until I can get myself together a little bit. Until I can find work." Krystal uttered a shaky laugh. "As long as you and Garrett will let me stay."

Garrett. Molly felt a flicker of panic. God, what would Garrett say? And how could she let Krystal stay indefinitely, not knowing how her sister and Garrett felt about each other? "I'll talk to him. I'm sure he won't mind."

"I hope not." Krystal took another swallow of beer. "It's your turn. Tell me how you came to be married to our stepbrother."

Pride kept Molly from wanting Krystal to know the truth about her marriage. "I always cared for Garrett. He came back and asked me, and I accepted because I realized I still care. I assume he cares, too," she lied, "or he wouldn't have asked me."

Krystal shook her head. "Mother would turn over in her grave."

"Mother did a lot of things I didn't approve of, either, Krys," Molly reminded, her smile bittersweet.

"That's true enough. What did Ian say?"

"He was shocked—"

"I'll bet," Krystal interrupted.

"—but he's come around, I think. Veronica is willing to wait and see, and Cindy adores Garrett."

"She would." Krystal swallowed another mouthful of beer. "And Garrett's family? What do they think? I'll bet Jon almost went into cardiac arrest."

"I don't know what they think," Molly confessed. "Jon and Ellen didn't come to the wedding."

Krystal's heavily lashed eyes widened in disbelief. "Ellen? Not Shiloh's mother, Ellen?"

"Yes," Molly told her. "They remarried. Garrett says they're very happy."

"Incredible! And Shiloh? Did she show up?"

Molly nodded. "She brought me the most gorgeous negligee..." Her voice trailed away, but Krystal didn't notice.

"What's Shiloh doing these days?" she asked, then added, "The little bitch."

Molly couldn't help smiling. Shiloh had rubbed Krystal the wrong way from the very first day she'd arrived to spend the summer with Jon. Almost the same age as Krystal, Shiloh hadn't been intimidated in the least by Krys's superior attitude. The two older girls had butted heads all summer, and not once had Krystal bested Garrett's pretty, dark-haired sister. The ultimate example of the iron fist in the velvet glove, Shiloh had a way of getting what she wanted without resorting to anything so crass as arguing. Named after the battle fought in Ellen's beloved state of Tennessee, because Ellen and Jon had fought bitterly throughout the pregnancy, Shiloh fit her name. She consistently won battles and beat down all problems with sweetness and logic.

"Shiloh owns her own French restaurant in Chattanooga. It's very fancy, very expensive, and she's getting very rich," Molly said.

"Figures," Krystal grumbled.

"She's worked hard for her success, Krys." *Unlike you, sister dear, who think you have to depend on your body to get what you want.*

"Did she ever get married?" There was keen interest in Krystal's eyes.

"No. She says she has no intention of becoming another divorce statistic."

"She always did think she was better than everyone else," Krystal said, pouring more beer into the glass. She sighed, satisfied, for the time being, with the gossip she'd heard. "Jet lag is catching up with me. Are you sure you and Garrett don't mind my staying?"

"I can't imagine that he'd turn anyone out under the circumstances," Molly said noncommittally.

Krystal's eyes held a thoughtful look. "It's going to be hard being around him so much."

The confession made Molly draw a deep breath. Krystal had broached the subject, so maybe now was the time to get to the bottom of things. "Why will it be hard, Krys? You say you love Freddy, and whatever was between you and Garrett was over a long time ago, wasn't it?"

For an instant, Krystal looked surprised. "Well, yes. Of course, it was, but I really loved him back then, Molly. We were...you know...?"

"Sleeping together." It was a statement, not a question.

To her credit, Krystal looked embarrassed. She shrugged. "You can't imagine how painful it was for me when he started seeing Linda."

Molly wasn't interested in hearing any more. The desire she'd felt for Garrett earlier was cheapened by Krystal's confession, and she wondered again if he'd compared her to her sister...and every other woman he'd had while they made love. Pushing her chair away from the table, she stood.

"I'm sorry," Krystal said, getting up from her chair. "I just don't want him to hurt you. He'll make you think you're the only woman in the world for him, but when someone else comes along who catches his eye, it'll all be over.''

Molly brushed aside her sister's explanation. ''I don't want to hear any more.''

Krystal nodded in agreement. ''You're right. I shouldn't have told you. I feel terrible.''

''No. It's all right.'' Molly ran her hand through her hair, suddenly overcome with weariness. ''Look, we can talk some more tomorrow, but I'm bushed right now. Let's go to bed.''

Krystal rose. ''Yeah. Me, too.''

They turned out the kitchen lights and went upstairs together. It wasn't until Molly was in bed, tossing in the heat once more that she realized Krystal had calmed down one set of worries and stirred up another. Molly had been concerned that there might be some old feelings left between Krystal and Garrett . . . some reason for her to be jealous of them. Evidently, that wasn't true...at least on her sister's part.

But Krystal's confession and warning had only fueled Molly's other worries: that if she did manage to attract him, she wouldn't be interesting enough or woman enough to hold him.

''What am I going to do, Silvie?'' she whispered into the night. Outside, the wind chimes tinkled, and the soft sound of Silvie's laughter mocked her, telling her without words that she'd have to figure it out on her own. . . .

* * *

In his room, Garrett smoked and waited. What in the sweet hell was Krystal doing here? He didn't buy her story about leaving Freddy and having no place to go—not for a minute. Not that he didn't believe the guy would dump her, bitch that she was, but she was bound to have friends—rich friends—she could dupe into putting her up for a while. People like Krystal were like cats. No matter how far the fall, they always landed on their feet.

No, there was some other reason she'd come, and it would take him a while to figure it out. If he had to hazard a guess, he'd say it was to weasel money out of Molly…or him, now that she knew he was paying the bills. Maybe it was to give Molly a hard time…to make her feel inferior the way he remembered she'd done in the past. Or, maybe, learning that he'd married her sister, Krystal had come to cause trouble, to get back at him because he'd warned his best friend, Don, about her after he'd caught them in bed together.

Restlessly, he rose, lit a cigarette, and went to the double doors that led to the gallery. A fitful, desultory breeze filtered through the wind chimes. The sound, as almost everything he came into contact with lately, reminded him of Molly. She'd been the one who insisted the wind chimes hang there when she'd come to Rambler's Rest as a girl. And they'd been there ever since. Funny, how such a small thing had become a part of his life, a part of the plantation's history…like Molly herself.

She was a good wife. She took care of the house and him with ease, and if he had any complaints so far, it was with his own behavior toward her. He was punishing her for something that wasn't her fault. It wasn't her fault that he found himself wanting to spend more time with her than he knew was good for him.

You're scared, Rambler. Admit it. You're scared that you're gonna fall for her despite all your good intentions. You're scared that she'll use you the way Lacey did. That she's already used you, and you like it.

He was scared. He was in over his head and scared to death that Molly, the one woman in the world he should stay away from was the only woman in the world who'd gotten under his skin. She'd already become such an integral part of his life, that he couldn't imagine her not being there. And now, here was Krystal. There was something almost...ominous about her arrival, he thought, drawing on the cigarette. Why had she come now, when things between him and Molly were still so unsettled?

He didn't want any trouble between him and Molly. He'd wondered about his reasons when he realized how much he'd missed her over the weekend. He'd been thinking about her when he'd seen Tut McClannahan and found out that he had some good quarter horses for sale. Having taught Molly to ride, he knew how much she loved the animals. He'd bought them on sight—in anticipation of her pleasure.

When he'd gotten back, he hadn't been disappointed, either in Molly's reaction to the horses, or in his reaction to her. He'd been so glad to see her that kissing her hello had been as natural as breathing. The feel of her body next to his and the softness of her lips made him realize how much he wanted her. The interesting thing was that Molly appeared to want him, too, so what was the use of denying themselves?

Call it lust. Call it desire, but whatever it was that bound them was undeniable. Today had been sort of a landmark in their strange relationship, a turning point, and he didn't want to go back to the way things had been.

Hell, he thought, grinding the cigarette out in a brass ashtray that sat beside his bed, he might as well face facts. He was falling for Molly. Falling for the woman whose sister had cheated on him and whose mother had taken his family for everything they were worth.

A new thought came to him out of left field. What if Krystal had come back to help Molly figure out some way to get back at him? Garrett kneaded the tight muscles at the back of his neck. *You're getting fanciful. Worse than Aunt Lisbet.*

Still, it was something to consider. What was he going to do about his feelings...and about Krystal? How could he keep her from poisoning Molly's mind with lies about him?

Through the open doors, carried on the soft summer breeze, came the tinkling sound of the wind chimes and the unmistakable sound of a young girl's teasing laughter.

It seemed to take an eternity, but Molly was almost asleep when she heard the door click shut. Instantly awake, she sat up in bed, her heart hammering in her throat. The shadowy figure of a man stood near the door...a familiar figure.

"Garrett," she whispered. "What are you doing here?"

In response, he crossed the room and sat down on the bed, sliding his arms around her and pulling her close. "We have some unfinished business, *Petite*," he told her huskily. He tangled his fingers through her hair and tugged her head back, covering her lips with his marauding mouth.

Until Garrett, Molly hadn't known how exciting a rough touch could be. He wasn't hurting her; he'd never hurt her, but whenever they were together, there was an element of desperation in his touch, in his kisses, that kept the gentleness at bay.

Molly reveled in it. When she'd made love before, she'd felt inadequate. Lacking. But with Garrett, it was as if he couldn't wait, couldn't get enough of her. The thought, the possibility that it was true, was like an aphrodisiac, urging her to be more daring, more adventuresome, more...than she'd ever felt she could be.

Like now.

Desire curled inside her, brushing aside the last vestige of sleep and banishing her fear. He was kindling to her fire, part to her counterpart, beat to her heart . . . and the man who had once been her sister's lover.

The reminder crept insidiously into her mind, destroying her passion the way Garrett's touch destroyed her inhibitions, and leaving cold where heat had been. She brought her hands up and pushed against his chest, tearing her mouth from his.

"Stop," she panted, holding him away from her.

Garrett's eyes glittered in the pale light of the moon. "Why?" he asked. "We both want it."

What could she say? She couldn't tell him that she couldn't make love with him because she was afraid he was comparing her to her sister, or that the picture she had of the two of them making love in her mind left her feeling sick. "I can't," she said.

"Why?"

"Krystal is in the next room."

"So? We're married."

"I know. But I can't."

Garrett was still for long moments. When he spoke, there was a hint of something in his voice that, if she didn't know better, sounded like sadness. "She's been telling you things about me again, hasn't she?"

Molly shook her head. "Nothing that she hasn't said before," she told him truthfully. "Or that I didn't already know."

"Like what?"

Molly tried to keep her voice light, unconcerned. "Like you slept with her best friend and broke Krystal's heart."

"And you believe that?"

A memory, a fragment of something vitally important to this conversation flitted through Molly's mind, just out of reach. "I remember her being upset when the two of you broke up."

Garrett wanted to tell Molly that Krystal had been upset because he had ruined her chances of snaring Don Ramsay by revealing her true colors. But something—male pride, maybe, or that hurt, vulnerable part of him that wanted her blind trust—stopped him. He released his hold on her, but smoothed his hand down her tangled hair. "Yeah," he said, "she was upset, all right."

Something in his voice caused her a moment's pause. "What are you saying?"

Garrett rose and went to the door, where he turned back to her. "I'm not saying anything, babe. You have to figure out the truth for yourself."

"What does that mean?"

"It means that if you want me, you know where I am."

As suddenly as he'd come, he was gone, leaving Molly to her thoughts.

It was almost three in the morning when she was on the fringes of sleep, when the memory of Mavis Davenport's words seeped into her mind, causing her eyes to fly open in remembrance. That night at the Waverly, Mavis had said something about Krystal being the one to cheat on Garrett—with *his* best friend. Molly had wondered about it at the time, but with trying to cope with her day-to-day routine and a new husband, it had gotten shuffled to the back of her mind. Is that what Garrett meant when he said she'd have to figure out the truth for herself? Why hadn't he just told her his side of things?

"Never forget a man's pride, darlin'. Mess with a man's pride and you got a whole heap of trouble." Liz's words of advice, advice Molly hadn't thought about since her mother gave it to her when she was sixteen and having boyfriend problems, came back with a vengeance.

Instinct told Molly that at least once, her mother had been right. She'd seen that male pride in her father, and heard Veronica complain about it enough to know that it was real and that it was often hard to deal with. Was that the problem? Was Garrett's pride standing in the way? Did he want her to believe him without having to explain himself?

Molly rolled to her side and punched her pillow. If the truth were known, neither her sister nor her husband had sterling reputations, and at that moment, she was so tired and confused, she didn't know what—or whom—to believe.

Worrying about who to believe was the first thing on Molly's mind when she awoke the next morning. She looked at the clock and saw that it was almost ten. Ten! She hadn't slept this late in ages, she thought, throwing back the sheet and climbing off the high bed. She wondered what Garrett had done for breakfast. And Krystal! She had company—her first as Mrs.

Jonathan Garrett Rambler—and she'd slept in, for heaven's sake!

When she got downstairs, the kitchen was littered with dirty dishes and remnants of pancakes and sausage. Neither Krystal nor Garrett was anywhere to be seen. Molly looked at the mess and decided that at least Garrett had eaten something before he went to work. And Krystal had never been an early riser. She was probably still in bed.

Molly fixed herself a short stack of pancakes and some fresh coffee, but found she couldn't eat. The coffee was bitter, and just looking at the syrup and butter congealing on her plate made her nauseous. Swallowing hard, she scraped the whole mess into the garbage disposal. It wasn't the same eating without Garrett. She'd never thought she'd get used to sitting across the table from someone who didn't pay any attention to her, but she had. Eating breakfast alone was...lonely.

Rising, she set about cleaning up the kitchen. She found the note near the box of pancake mix. Written in Krystal's flowing scrawl, the message was brief and to the point. She had fixed Garrett's breakfast—sorry about the mess—and Garrett had agreed to take her into town to buy some art supplies. They would be back by noon or so.

Molly crumpled the note and stared blindly out into the bright sunshine. Her man-eating sister had fixed breakfast for *her* husband, and had somehow talked Garrett into running errands...something Molly hadn't had the guts to ask him to do for her—or with her. And Garrett, who hadn't taken a day off since their wedding, obviously had no problem with the arrangement.

She, however, did.

Molly was still seething when Garrett's BMW pulled around the house and into the garage at the back. Fighting a feeling of sickness, she had prepared fried chicken, mashed some potatoes and fixed corn on the cob and sliced tomatoes for lunch. Molly had also made certain that she looked cool and attractive in her shorts and sandals.

Hearing their approach, she poured the gravy into the gravy boat and set it on the table as if she didn't care what they'd been doing. Then she heard Krystal's laughter. Nothing short of shackles could have kept Molly from turning to look out the window.

Garrett was carrying two large bags that bore the names of a local art supply store, and Krystal, dressed in a white silk blouse and a jade-green linen skirt that had Paris couture written all over it, walked—almost danced—along beside him.

Molly thought of her flash of memory the night before and wondered if Mavis had been right about Krystal cheating on Garrett. Molly also thought regretfully of how she'd sent Garrett away when he'd wanted to make love. Had she thrown away her last chance?

No, she vowed. She'd thrown away a chance, but not her last one. She wasn't going to let Krystal get the best of her this time. She was an adult now, and she knew what she wanted. She wanted Garrett.

The back door swung open, and Krystal preceded Garrett into the room. Molly turned to greet them, with what she hoped was a welcoming smile on her lips. Frowning, Garrett looked her over from head to toe. "Hi," she said.

"Hi," Krystal replied, drawing Molly's attention away from Garrett. "Did you find my note?"

"Yeah. Sorry I was such a sleepyhead. Thanks for taking care of my husband's breakfast." It gave Molly a great deal of satisfaction to remind Krystal of Garrett's status.

"Any time."

Over my dead body. Molly sneaked a peek at Garrett, who was setting Krystal's parcels in a corner of the kitchen floor. She looked back at her sister. "Did you find what you need?"

"Almost everything. I'm really anxious to get started painting again," Krystal said. "It's always been a restful thing for me to do."

Restful wasn't a word Molly would ever associate with Krystal, but she was glad her sister would have something to occupy her time. It meant she wouldn't have to entertain her. She had to admit that Krystal was highly talented and that if she'd been more inclined to work and less to play she might have had a very successful art career.

"That's great. Why don't you set up in the blue room," Molly suggested. "It has a northern exposure."

Krystal's smile appeared genuine. "Thanks, sis. That's a great idea."

Molly turned away to get some glasses. "Lunch is ready."

"Oh, Molly, I'm sorry," Krystal lamented with a pouting look, "but Garrett bought me lunch in town."

Chapter Ten

By the end of July, when Krystal's stay had dragged on a month, Molly was beginning to doubt in the existence of justice and the rewards of good living. Surely if justice were to be done and it was true that one reaped what one sowed, Krystal's stay would have ended by now. Molly had fought a daily battle to be kind to her sister, even though Krystal was driving her slowly insane...and driving a wedge between her and Garrett.

Besides her outrageous flirting with Garrett—which he accepted with good grace, but with no reciprocal passes that Molly could determine—Krystal never lifted a hand to do anything. Old habits did die hard, and Molly's urge to take over Krystal's chores was never far away. She had to remind herself daily that she wasn't going to let Krystal walk on her. But since she had to cook for herself and Garrett anyway, Molly did fix Krystal's meals and wound up cleaning the kitchen alone. However, she refused to clean her sister's room or do her laundry, which resulted in a mountain of dirty clothes that Krystal washed only out of necessity... fuming all the while that she was involved with her painting and had better things to do.

As if Molly didn't. Besides her usual household duties, she had volunteered earlier in the year to chair the annual Christmas on the Bayou Festival. Though the floating tours down the bayou were scheduled to start two weeks before Christmas, the time for an organizational meeting was rapidly approaching. A committee of landowners along Bayou Lafourche and city officials from Thibodaux, Houma and Raceland would be included in the initial meeting, where a schedule of festivities would be confirmed and new ideas would be introduced. Molly spent every spare minute racking her brain for novel schemes, but with the heat and lethargy that held her in its grip, she usually ended up falling asleep at the table.

If the truth were known, she wasn't feeling well. It was nothing she was able to put her finger on, until the day she checked the dates for an upcoming tour and dinner and realized she was over a week late.

She couldn't be late. Clutching the calendar, Molly sat down at the table and stared in disbelief. It was August first, and she should have started around the twenty-fifth of July. As regular as clockwork, Molly knew something was wrong. There was no way she could be pregnant. She and Garrett had only made love one time, and she'd had a period in June . . . not much of one and late, but, with the upheaval in her life, nothing was normal. At the time, she had sighed with relief and gone on about her business.

Molly laid the calendar down and stared blankly out a window across the room. Could she be pregnant? She gnawed her bottom lip. It was possible, anything was possible, but . . . What should she do? What would Garrett think? They hardly spoke anymore.

She admitted that much of the problem was her, not Garrett. As far as she could tell, he'd never once given either her or Krystal any reason to believe there were any lingering feelings from the past. On the contrary, Molly couldn't help remembering how he'd come to her bedroom the night of Krystal's arrival and how she'd turned him away. She remembered, too, that he'd told her that the next move was hers, a move she hadn't been able to make. It was as much Krystal's presence as what she'd told Molly about Garrett that stopped Molly from going to him. Her sister was intimidating, overbearing in subtle ways, and made Molly feel klutzy and frumpy.

But much to Molly's surprise, Krystal was working hard, putting in long hours at the easel. She was painstakingly copying the Landseer and the Bonheur to hone her skills, because if she got good enough, there was a man she knew in Paris who might be willing to show her work in his gallery.

So, while Molly sweltered in the heat, doing the thousand and one things it took to keep the house running smoothly, Krystal holed up in an air-conditioned room and worked at capturing the textures and nuances of Rambler's Rest's two original works of art. While Molly was wilted at day's end, Krystal looked as if she'd stepped off the pages of *Vogue*. It took all Molly's good grace to wish her sister luck with her painting and all her strength to keep from breaking beneath the burden of Krystal's presence in the house.

Molly was tired of being strong. She was just tired. But at least now, she knew why. Going to the back door, she looked out over the rose garden and the arbor where she and Garrett had said their wedding vows almost seven weeks ago. No one was around, so she allowed herself the luxury of a few tears, wondering how she would tell Garrett about the baby—if it was true she was pregnant—and how he would react.

Several times during the last few weeks, she'd caught him staring at her with an expression in his eyes she'd imagined to be something between tenderness and worry. She'd longed to go to him and tell him she was sorry she'd said no, that she wanted to sleep with him—more than that, she wanted to love him. But if she didn't manage to convince herself that she'd mistaken his look, the thought of Krystal always stopped her.

Molly wiped the tears from her eyes. She was tired of wimping out. She was tired of not knowing what to do. But no more. Her current situation called for action, not passivity.

"First things first."

The first thing she would do was see a doctor and confirm her suspicions; then, she would decide where to go from there.

Molly settled heavily into the lounge cushion...the same lounge cushion she and Garrett had almost made love on what seemed an eternity ago. In spite of the unrelenting heat, she'd sought out the gallery as a sort of penance, a reminder of what might have been. After three days of wondering about the outcome of her visit to the doctor, she knew.

Wearily, her gaze scanned the sky. Thunderheads were building toward the west, and an occasional burst of wind offered a brief respite from the heat. Though it looked like rain, Molly knew better than to get her hopes up. Dark clouds had gathered almost every day, and it had even rained twice, though the smattering of drops hardly settled the dust before the capricious wind blew the clouds somewhere else to dump their precious cargo.

The yard needed watering again, she thought, noticing how dead-looking the grass was. She felt the ridiculous sting of tears behind her eyelids and knew that, just like everything else in her life, her emotions were out of kilter. She was getting upset over dead grass, for crying out loud! But everything seemed to be dead or dying, including whatever it was that had been taking tentative root between her and Garrett. The doctor's news would no doubt finish that off, as well.

"I've gone and done it, now, Silvie," she said to the wind chimes. "I'm pregnant."

The bells seemed to sway in response, but not enough to make a sound.

Molly's mouth twisted. "Yeah. I know what you mean. I didn't know what to say, either." She raised a glass of orange juice in a salute, took a sip, and grimaced at its tartness. "Anyway, I'm going into my eighth week, and it looks as if I may not have a horrible time with morning sickness, so I'll probably be a blimp come fall."

Deep down, she was glad she was pregnant, but the uncertainty of Garrett's response kept her from fully appreciating the fact that they were going to have a baby. Instead of searching her mind for names, she searched it for ways to tell him…and came up empty-handed. And instead of feeling happy about the news, she felt sick.

That could be because you haven't had anything to eat all day, Molly.

Probably. And then, again, it could be the damnable heat. Maybe she'd go in and take a bath and a long nap before starting dinner. She would have to cook early tonight, because the Christmas on the Bayou meeting was scheduled for seven o'clock at the home of Jack Navarre, a local merchant.

Molly sighed. Chairing a meeting was the last thing she wanted to do—especially tonight, with her sister in tow. When Krystal had shown her completed paintings to a city councilman she'd once dated, he'd invited her to do the artwork for the publicity. Even though she knew Krystal would be excellent for the job, Molly had little doubt that her sister would monopolize the meeting and upstage her at every opportunity.

She started to get up, but activity near the bayou caught her attention. A woman with long dark hair darted from one tree to another, and a man in jeans and a short-sleeved, blue shirt followed. Molly saw him grab her by the arm and push her up against the trunk of an ancient sycamore. He kissed her, a lengthy kiss filled with passion.

A sick feeling churned inside Molly's stomach, and a sharp pain stabbed her heart. Krystal. Molly recognized the multicolored shirt as the one her sister had worn to breakfast. Still, it was hard to believe her eyes, especially since she'd kept a close watch on Garrett for signs of interest in her sister. So far she hadn't detected any. But who else, Molly thought with a sinking heart, could the man be, but her husband?

The bathwater was purposefully, blissfully cool... and getting colder. Molly had started off with tepid water and a froth of bubbles that evaporated as the water chilled beneath the slow pirouette of an oscillating fan. She had spent the better part of an hour in the tub, soaking, crying and replaying the scene she'd witnessed from the back gallery. Though it was hard to believe that Garrett would carry on an affair with her sister right under her nose, what else was she to think, under the circumstances?

Hoping that discretion truly was the better part of valor, Molly decided to bide her time and see what else transpired before she confronted either of them. An affair could only be kept secret indefinitely, and patience wasn't one of Krystal's attributes. Something was bound to give—and soon. In the meantime, Molly decided to keep her pregnancy secret. The baby was one part of her life that nothing could tarnish and no one could take away from her.

Already, her unborn child was changing her and her life.

Tiny blue veins were more visible in her breasts, which were fuller and tender to the touch. Her stomach was still flat, but, Molly could have sworn there was a subtle difference. For the first time since her suspicions had been confirmed, she felt a measure of comfort and peace knowing that Garrett's child was growing inside her. She dreaded leaving the peace and isolation of the bathroom and facing the world.

Outside, thunder rumbled, the sound coinciding with the grumbling of her empty stomach. Admitting that her too-brief idyll was over, Molly pulled the plug and stood, reaching for a peach-tinted towel hanging on a nearby bar. Simultaneously, a high-pitched, girlish giggle wafted through the air, and, without warning, the door burst open on a strong gust of wind. It banged against the wall and almost frightened Molly out of her wits.

"Silvie," Molly said aloud, "stop—"

Her voice broke off when she saw the figure in the hallway. Dripping wet, she stood there, the still-folded towel in her hands, her mouth an O of surprise as she stared into the equally shocked eyes of her husband.

Garrett couldn't help staring. His gaze moved from Molly's face and grazed her body... her bare body. Dear God, had she ever been more beautiful? Her legs were slender, shapely...her waist so small, her breasts so full. Had they always been so ripe looking? Had her nipples always been so dark? He remembered them as dusty pink, like the roses bordering the front lawn.

For the span of a dozen heartbeats, he feasted on the sight of her, before the towel fell, unfolded, to her knees, hiding her from his hungry eyes.

"Where have you been?" she asked, the words out before she could stop them. *So much for biding your time, Molly.*

Garrett's eyes narrowed. He plowed his fingers through his dark hair, that was sweaty and dusty. "Cutting hay. The last of it, if we don't get some rain."

Molly tried not to think of how sexy he looked standing there in his faded Levi's. She forced her mind to focus on the issue at hand. Now that she'd started the ball rolling, it would be better to get whatever was going on out in the open, even if it led to a quarrel. Garrett owed her an explanation.

"Where?" she asked.

"Across the highway."

"You weren't out back—along the bayou an hour or so ago?"

Garrett shifted his weight to one leg and propped his hands on his lean hips, the picture of masculine arrogance and insolence. "Do we have a hay field out back?" he retaliated with cool sarcasm. "What is this, Molly? Twenty questions?"

Should she believe him? Molly's teeth worried her bottom lip. No. She'd come this far, she couldn't back off now. Defiantly, she raised her chin to a belligerent angle and hugged the towel against her body. "I saw Krystal kissing a man out back."

How could Molly think he was interested in her sister, when it was all he could do to keep from ripping away the towel and taking her right there in the middle of the bathroom? Garrett couldn't stop the wanting, even though he felt like a fool. Molly had made it very clear that he held no great interest to her.

Damning his inability to put her out of his mind, he stripped off his sweat-stained T-shirt, rolled it in a ball, and tossed it to the floor. Calmly, he shut the door, cloistering them in the intimacy of the small room. "Let me guess," he said, with a crooked twist of his lips as he folded his arms over his chest. "You thought it was me."

Hearing him voice her suspicion, Molly was suddenly afraid she'd made a grave error in judgment.

"Why?" he asked, before she could answer. Reaching out, he lifted her chin. Standing in the tub, she was forced to meet him eye to eye.

"Why?" he asked, his breath a cool vapor against her hot cheeks. "Why would you believe that I feel anything for her when I've done my damnedest to stay away from her."

Molly stared into his blue eyes and could have sworn she detected pain in his voice.

"How can you be sure it was Krystal?"

"I recognized her clothes."

Garrett's thumb slid over her bottom lip. "And did you recognize my clothes?"

Molly could hardly think, he was so close. Then she remembered. "The shirt I saw was blue," she said breathlessly.

Garrett released his hold on her chin and bent to pick up his shirt. His *black* T-shirt. Relief, heady and sweet, eddied through her as she realized that Garrett wasn't the man she'd seen with Krystal beneath the trees. She owed him an apology, and...

Reaching out, he lifted her from the tub, stopping all thought. His hands were warm against the wet coolness of her flesh. Warm and strong...

"Molly! Are you in there? What were you laughing about?" Krystal's strident voice sliced through the moment like a surgeon's scalpel, cutting through the dream to reality.

"Go away, Krystal," Garrett said in a rough voice. He released Molly and, with his gaze holding hers, deliberately took the towel from her numb fingers. Just as deliberately, he bent and pressed a hot, open-mouthed kiss to each breast, his tongue rasping against each turgid nipple. Her legs threatened to give way, and she gripped his forearm to steady herself. Then, without a word, he straightened and wrapped the towel around her, sarong style, tucking the ends over the swell of her breasts.

"The past is past, *Petite*," he said, "and I did a lot of things I regret. But I don't cheat at cards, and I won't cheat on my wife. If I ever want out of this marriage—for any reason—I'll be up-front with you. I won't sneak around."

For some reason she believed him. She still didn't know what to think about his past affair with her sister, but there was no denying the sincerity in his voice and eyes. The wind chimes sang merrily as a gusty breeze floated through the open window, blowing a strand of Molly's hair across her lips.

Garrett reached out and gently pulled the fiery hair from where it had caught on the moistness of her mouth. "I think Silvie is trying to play matchmaker," he said, dead serious.

So he, as well as Krystal, had heard the laughter.

He brushed her cheekbone with the backs of his fingers and let them trail down to the firm upper portion of her breasts. "You know what? I think maybe it's working."

Molly drew in a tremulous breath.

Garrett sighed heavily. "Go see what your sister wants, *Petite*," he said huskily. "I'm gonna take a cold shower and cool off."

Molly wished the heat would relax its hold. As she'd expected, the wind had blown and thunder had rolled, but no rain had fallen in the area. Which was a pity, since the Navarreses had decided to have the meeting outside. There were almost twenty people present—including two city councilmen, the heads of three

Chambers of Commerce, one reporter...and Mavis Davenport. Actually, Molly thought as she sipped at her soda and used the handful of papers she held as a fan, everyone else was talking and she was trying to keep cool.

It was interesting watching the interplay among the people present. Krystal, who was a bit tipsy, flirted with every man there; Lois Navarre tried to make everyone comfortable; the politicians made their requisite rounds; Mavis Davenport did what she did best, asking hundreds of questions but leaving the newlywed Ramblers alone; and Garrett sat at Molly's side as a dutiful husband should.

Mavis did, however, gush over Krystal, who told her about her last few years abroad—including her marriage to Freddy, and her possible affiliation with a Paris gallery but omitting information about her possible divorce. Finally, after two hours of give-and-take, there was a lull in the conversation. As usual, Krystal decided to make the most of it.

"May I have another tequila sunrise, please?" she asked Jack Navarre in her sweetest tone.

"Sure thing," he said, jumping to his feet and throwing his arm around her shoulders as they headed toward the house. Lois Navarre watched them go, a speculative look in her eyes.

And no wonder. Krystal had been flirting with Jack ever since she'd arrived. It didn't matter that he was in his late forties. He was attractive and attentive, the two qualities it took to snag her interest. Since her sister had been hitting the alcohol pretty hard, Molly was worried about what might happen if Krystal got Jack alone.

The need to intervene weighed heavily on Molly's already drooping shoulders. At least if she went inside to monitor their behavior, she could enjoy the air-conditioning for a moment.

"Wait, Krys," she called. "I need some more tea." Molly stood, and a wave of dizziness washed over her. She had to grab the back of a nearby chair to steady herself. Luckily the feeling passed quickly.

She'd almost reached the patio door when Garrett grabbed her arm in a gesture she realized she'd missed the last two months. "Are you all right?"

Molly looked up into blue eyes that held definite concern and felt her world sway. She lifted a hand to her throbbing temple and tried to smile. "I'm fine. It's just so hot." She looked toward the doors where Jack and Krystal had disappeared.

"What is it?" Garrett asked.

Her eyes were filled with worry. "Krystal," she whispered. "She's had too much to drink, and so has Jack. I'm afraid she'll do something we'll all regret."

"They're both adults," Garrett reminded softly. "And you're not Krystal's keeper. She's the one responsible for her actions, not you."

"Lois Navarre is my friend."

The simple sentence said more than she realized. Without another word, Garrett let her go. Anxious to get inside, Molly turned—too quickly. Her head wheeled and spun, and the patio doors danced in front of her. She reached out for the handle, but couldn't find the strength to slide back the door.

Through the glass, she saw Krystal draw Jack's head down to hers. Molly wanted to scream at her sister to stop, but she couldn't speak while she was trying to keep the house from spinning. With a sharp cry of distress, she felt her hand slip and her legs buckle. She went down ... slipping into a whirling abyss of darkness.

When Molly woke up, her bedside clock said seven-thirty. Exhausted with the heat and her inner turmoil, she'd slept away the night. She realized that she must have fainted when she'd seen Krystal kiss Jack. Somehow, though she had no memory of it, Garrett had brought her home, to her own bed. Her head ached, and her shoulder hurt where she'd fallen, but she felt more rested than she had in several days.

What had Garrett thought? Would he think she'd fainted from the heat? She eased from the bed, wondering if he had already gone to the hay field and if Krystal had fixed breakfast.

When Molly got downstairs, Garrett, dressed in jodhpurs and a white shirt, was sitting at the table reading the paper and drinking a cup of coffee. She glanced toward the back door and saw that the horses were saddled and tied to the hitching post near the barn. Evidently, he had a morning ride planned for the two of them. Even though the idea pleased her, she paused in the doorway, feeling almost shy after her fainting spell.

Garrett looked up from his paper. "Good morning," he said somberly. "How are you feeling?"

"Fine." Molly went to the refrigerator. "Were you planning for us to ride this morning?" she asked over her shoulder.

"If you feel like it."

"It sounds wonderful," she said, pouring herself some orange juice. "Where's Krystal?"

"Gone."

Molly turned to face him. "Gone? Where?"

Garrett lifted his shoulders in a careless shrug. "I don't know, and I don't care as long as it's far away from here."

Molly carried her glass to the table and sat down across from him. "What happened?"

"I asked—" Garrett paused, and his eyes glittered with anger and defiance "—no, dammit, I *told* her to leave, which she did an hour ago. I'm sorry if that makes you angry."

"It doesn't make me angry," Molly told him with a shake of her head, "but why?"

"Because all she was doing was using us until a better situation came along. I was tired of the extra work she was causing you and sick of her putting you down. Not to mention the fact that she made a fool of herself at the Navarres's last night."

A pleased feeling spread through Molly. She hadn't realized that Garrett noticed Krystal's sly digs, but he obviously had. And his actions proved that he cared for her...at least to some degree. Molly couldn't hide the smile that curved her lips. "Thanks." She stood eagerly, heading for the refrigerator. "Have you had breakfast?"

"I'm not very hungry."

That surprised her. Garrett was always hungry.

"What about you?" he asked.

"I'm starving," she said, taking a roll of sausage from the refrigerator. "I didn't eat much all day yesterday."

"Do you think that's why you fainted?" He asked the question casually, but under the circumstances, Molly found it suspect.

Molly stopped what she was doing and looked at him, trying to gauge his feelings. "Probably," she agreed. "That and the heat."

"Then there's no truth in what the paper says?"

"The paper?" She frowned. "There's something in the paper about my fainting at the Navarres's?" Then she remembered. "Ah. Mavis—right?"

Garrett kept a close watch on her reactions. "Right."

Molly returned her attention to the sausage. "I thought she would have learned a lesson from her last encounter with us. So what does she have to say?"

"That you're pregnant."

Garrett's words, followed by the clatter of her dropped knife, fell like lead into the silence of the kitchen. Molly heard his chair scrape against the floor as he pushed away from the table, heard his booted feet carry him to where she stood, felt his hands close around her shoulders.

He turned her around to face him and lifted her chin until their eyes met. There was anguish in Molly's gaze. The emotion in Garrett's was indecipherable. "Is it true?"

Why deny it? The world would know soon enough. "Yes."

Garrett expelled a deep breath, as if he'd been holding it in anticipation of her answer. He dragged a hand down his whisker-stubbled face, and, without another word, started for the back door.

Molly didn't know what she'd expected. Anger, maybe. Or regret. Anything but this cold, controlled, *emotionless* acceptance. Fury rose inside her. Running after him, she grabbed his arm the way he had hers so many times in the past. "Well, thanks a heap for asking me how I feel about having a baby—your baby," she cried, her eyes blazing with anger. "Better yet, Garrett, why don't you tell me how you feel?"

Very gently, he pried her fingers loose. "I feel sorry," he said, and left her standing in the middle of the kitchen floor, her anger gone, her dreams and hopes going out the door with him.

Stunned, she watched him cross the yard to the barn. By the time he reached the horses, tears were streaming down her cheeks. He was sorry she was having his baby. Pressing her palm to the pane of glass, as if by doing this she could somehow touch him, Molly watched Garrett mount the gelding and gallop across the field.

How could he just walk away from her? It was his baby too. Misery gave way to rekindled anger. Damn him! She'd had enough. She wasn't going to let him act as if their marriage and their baby was a game of cards and he'd drawn a bad hand. This was a life they were talking about. Three lives. Garrett might not be used to talking about how he felt, or what was going on inside him, but he was darn well going to tell her.

Flinging open the door, she ran across the yard and wrenched the reins free from the hitching post. Placing her tennis shoe in the stirrup, she scrambled onto the mare's broad back. Clicking her tongue and digging her heels into the horse's sides, Molly sped through the open gate and across the pasture after him.

Garrett, still shaking, heard her coming. He pulled his horse to a stop at the wooded area bordering the bayou and, turning in the saddle, watched her race toward him. She shouldn't be riding, should she? Leaning low across the saddle horn, her hair flying out behind her like crimson streamers fluttering in the wind, she looked wild and free and . . . furious, he realized, as she drew nearer. Lord, but she was gorgeous when she was angry.

Bracing himself for the oncoming storm, Garrett dismounted and tied the gelding to a French mulberry bush. In a matter of seconds, Molly was reining the mare in. The horse skidded to a stop, and before it was completely still, Molly was off its back and striding toward him. Was she crazy? Didn't she know that was a dangerous stunt?

Garrett stalked toward her.

"That's a damn fool trick in your condition," he growled in tandem with Molly's impassioned, "How dare you say you're sorry I'm pregnant, you no-account slime?"

As each other's statement registered, they spoke simultaneously the second time.

"What do you care about my condition?" Molly's breasts heaved with rage.

"Slime?" Garrett's nostrils flared with fury.

They eyed each other warily.

"How dare you say you're sorry about this baby." She doubled up a small fist and struck him in the middle of his chest. "How *dare* you! I suppose you're sorry you married me, too."

Garrett's fingers circled her waist. "I'm not sorry about marrying you and I'm not sorry about you having a baby," he growled. "I'm sorry for the way it happened."

"The way it happened?" Molly's anger dissipated in the face of her old adversary—inadequacy. She shook her head. Tears glittered in her green eyes, and her bottom lip trembled. "I realize that I'm not worldly or experienced...but I sure as heck didn't hear any complaints at the time."

Garrett saw the old insecurity in her eyes. She thought he was displeased with her. He swore, shaking her slightly. "Of course you didn't hear any complaints, you little idiot, which is why I got so carried away that I forgot to show any concern for you. I'll never forgive myself for being so rough and inconsiderate."

Molly blinked as the truth became crystal clear. "Is that why you were so angry? You were mad at yourself?"

"Yeah." He snorted with disgust and turned away. "Garrett Rambler, great lover, roughs up his wife on their wedding night."

Molly grabbed his arm and turned him around. "You didn't rough me up," Molly said, longing to relieve his pain. "You were always gentle." Her lips quirked in a half smile. "Impatient, maybe, but you never hurt me. Not once. You never have." Her voice dropped a decibel. "I thought I'd disappointed you."

"What?"

She lifted one shoulder in a self-effacing shrug. "I didn't know what else to blame your behavior on."

Garrett kneaded the tight muscles at the nape of his neck. Lord, what a mess he'd made of things. Molly had been right. He should have talked to her, told her what he was feeling, and none of this would have happened. "You're right. I am a slime."

Molly smiled. Reaching out, she started unbuttoning his shirt. "I'm sorry. That was uncalled for."

"What are you doing?"

Her hands moved around the waistband of his pants, working his shirt free. "Making the next move."

"Making the next move? What do you...Molly..." he moaned as her fingers deftly unfastened his jodhpurs.

"We can't keep going on the way we have been, Garrett, and you told me the night I turned you down, that the next move was mine. Well, I'm making it."

She leaned forward and trailed a string of kisses down his chest to his navel where her tongue dipped briefly. Lifting her head, she smiled—a sexy, bewitching smile that would have done Krystal proud. "If I do anything wrong, you just let me know."

Her hand slid beneath the elastic waistband of his shorts. "So far, *Petite*," he hissed from between clenched teeth, "you're doing just fine."

Chapter Eleven

Garrett had been gone to Atlantic City for almost a week, and Molly was miserable. He'd taken the ruby and diamond jewelry—the only pieces along with the ring he'd given her that Jon had managed to salvage from the divorce. Jon had called, saying he knew someone who seemed interested in buying them. Though Molly knew this was a preferable alternative to using the paintings as collateral for the rice and crawfish farm, she still hated Garrett's being away. She'd become used to his presence in the big house, and ever since she'd seduced him at the bayou more than two weeks ago, she'd become used to him in her bed.

Life had definitely improved since that day. She hadn't been plagued with morning sickness at all, though she still tried to rest during the hottest part of the afternoons. Sometimes Garrett joined her, but on those days sleep was the furthest thing from her mind. She still caught him looking at her as if he was trying to figure her out, still had to force him to tell her what was going on. No words of love or devotion had passed his lips during the times they made wildly glorious love to each other, but Molly was content.

And, she was excited. Garrett was coming home, and an unseasonal cool front was moving down from the north. The temperature and barometric pressure had been dropping steadily the last hour, and according to the meteorologists, record lows would be set during the night. There were tornado watches statewide. The promise of a cool spell made Molly's life complete. She was afraid, though, that the storms might delay Garrett's flight, which was due to land in New Orleans at nine in the evening. She wanted him home on time. She missed him.

To help the time go faster, she had invited her dad and Veronica over for dinner. After finishing the meal—during which she'd answered a million questions about how she and Garrett were getting along and how they both felt about becoming parents—Molly served pie and coffee in the parlor.

"It's getting chilly," Veronica said, as Molly poured coffee from the silver service into a delicate Spode cup.

Ian added a spoonful of sugar to his chicory-laced brew. "It's the wind. It's getting strong out there."

Veronica looked worried. "Do you think we should get home to the girls?"

"Probably," Ian told her with an indulgent smile. "But we do have time for a cup of coffee, Ronnie."

"Yes, dear," Veronica said with mock servility. She cast a troubled glance out the window, where the trees were being whipped to and fro. "Do you want me to close the windows, Molly?"

"Not yet, thanks." Molly smiled and drew a deep breath. "It feels good to me."

"Humor her," Ian teased. "She's expecting. What time did you say Garrett was getting in to New Orleans?"

"Nine o'clock." Molly's gaze followed her stepmother's. "I'm beginning to wonder if they'll cancel the flight."

"Why don't you call the airline?" Ian suggested, adding dryly, "Then you'll know whether or not to start worrying at ten."

"Ian!" Veronica chided.

"Good idea, Daddy."

In a matter of seconds, the airline's number was ringing.

"Hello. I'm calling to see if the flight scheduled to arrive in New Orleans at nine p.m. is on time. It's been canceled? Yes, I understand. Can you tell me if Garrett Rambler has been transferred to another flight? Rambler. Garrett Rambler. What?" Molly's startled gaze flew to her father's. Her heart sank, and a terrible feeling of foreboding enveloped her. "Are you sure? All right, thank you."

She hung up the phone and looked from Ian to Veronica. "The flight has been canceled, but the woman said that Garrett had never booked on it. When I talked to him yesterday, he told me he was coming in at nine tonight.''

Ian and Veronica exchanged concerned glances. ''Maybe you got the wrong airline,'' her father suggested.

The relief that spread through Molly left her feeling weak. She shoved her heavy hair away from her face in a distracted gesture. ''Yes. That must be it,'' she said, thumbing through the Yellow Pages again.

Twenty minutes later, Molly had exhausted every airline in the book, and no one had Garrett Rambler listed as a passenger. A sick feeling gripped her.

As Molly replaced the receiver, a gust of wind howled through the darkening evening. It whistled round the corners of the house and forced its way through the open windows, pushing aside everything in its path. The crewel curtains billowed out, pulling the rod loose and tangling the fabric in the turned legs of a marble-topped stand. It crashed to the floor, taking a vase of fresh-cut flowers with it and shattering the lead crystal into a million irreparable pieces.

Before Molly and the others could do more than gasp in shock, the wind swirled through the room, sweeping the Bonheur from its place over the mantle and sending it tumbling to the floor. The sight of the painting landing on its corner and the sound of the antique frame cracking, galvanized Ian and Veronica into action. Rising almost simultaneously, they went to the windows, shutting out the approaching storm, while Molly moved stiffly toward the painting, her brain denying what her eyes were seeing.

Bending, she stooped and picked up the picture, turning the frame to the back. The canvas was new, not dull with age.

"Molly?" Ian said, seeing the horrified look on her face. "What is it?"

Still holding the painting, she met his gaze as steadily as possible. She couldn't tell her father what she suspected. "The frame's ruined," she said truthfully, "and it's very old."

Ian looked relieved. "Well, it's a shame, but not the end of the world. I'm sure you can find another in an antique shop."

"Yeah," Molly said, placing the damaged picture on the floor. She was suddenly eager to have them gone so that she could check the Landseer. "I'm sure you're right." She glanced out the window. "It's getting pretty rough out there. Maybe you two should head out."

Veronica looked out at the rolling clouds. "She's right, Ian. We'd better start home. Why don't you come with us, Molly? I hate to leave you here alone with those storms headed this way."

Molly kissed her stepmother's cheek. "Thanks, Ronnie, but I'll be fine. The house and I have weathered plenty of bad weather."

Veronica smiled. "You have, at that."

Ian draped his arm over his wife's shoulders. "You hang in there and don't worry about Garrett. He's probably holed up in a motel somewhere, waiting for the weather to clear so he can come on home.''

Molly nodded, but couldn't quite make herself believe that scenario. She helped them get their things together and waved them off from the safety of the porch. As they pulled out of the driveway, the rain started, falling from the sky in a gray torrent. Going straight to the mantel, she took the Landseer from its place of honor. She turned it over and saw that it, too, was a fake. Numb with shock, she carried the dessert dishes to the kitchen, and cleaned up the broken vase, trying to control the dark thoughts that were scrambling through her brain.

Impossible.

Both the Bonheur and the Landseer were gone, replaced with copies. Excellent copies.

"Krystal," Molly said aloud. "Krystal did it for Garrett."

Even as she said it, Molly thought of how perfectly it fit. Garrett had wanted to use the paintings as collateral. She had refused. Soon afterward, Krystal had come and begun copying the originals. Just a week ago, Garrett had made her leave—so he said—and now he was gone and the paintings had been switched.

Garrett and Krystal must have planned the whole thing. The possibility that she'd stumbled onto a clever scam and been taken in by Garrett broke her heart. She didn't want to believe it, but what other answer could there be?

Okay, you don't want to believe that Garrett is guilty, so who else could have taken them? Who else needed the money?

Molly thought for a moment. "Krystal," she said again, knowing there was no one else.

But do you really believe that your own sister would steal from you?

In a heartbeat.

Why?

Why? Why would Krystal do something so devious? So wrong? A snippet of conversation from the past played through Molly's mind. When Krystal had called from Greece, she'd said she and Freddy were broke, and now that they'd split up, she no doubt needed the money. That much was logical. But it was still hard for Molly to accept the fact that her own sister would steal from her.

Isn't it easier to think it was Krystal than it is to believe it was Garrett?

Oh, yes, that was much easier. But, Krystal didn't seem like the type to choreograph something this slick. The truth was Molly didn't think Krystal was bright enough to plan a scheme this clever. The only two things Krys was capable of planning were her wardrobe and her next affair.

Someone must have masterminded it. Who?

Who? Molly massaged her throbbing temples and thought again of the man she'd seen with Krystal near the bayou. She'd wanted to believe it was someone else, not Garrett, but . . .

Oh, what was the use? Molly thought, leaping to her feet. Why waste her energy trying to figure out who the culprit was? One thing was certain. Whether or not Garrett and Krystal were in cahoots, he was bound to show up at some time. After all, he owned the place.

Her mind reeling with fatigue and anxiety, Molly started for bed. She was halfway up the stairs, when the electricity flickered once and died, plunging the house into total darkness.

Wonderful! she thought with a weary sigh. At least she knew her way around the house blindfolded. Turning, she made her way through the dark house to the kitchen pantry where she kept a lantern and some matches. Striking a sulfurous tip, she lit the wick of the oil lamp and carried it upstairs.

Alone in the familiarity of her bedroom, she turned out the lantern and curled up beneath the covers. She didn't mean to rehash everything. And she didn't mean to cry, but then she hadn't meant to fall in love with Garrett, either.

Something awakened Molly from a dream. Probably the quiet. She didn't know how long she'd slept, but the storm had worn itself out, at least for the moment. She wondered what time it was, but knew she wouldn't be able to see the clock in the darkness. She was too tired to relight the lantern. Besides, she'd rather try to reconstruct the dream in her mind. It seemed important that she try to remember it.

Molly closed her eyes and pulled what she could from her sleep-fogged mind. She and Garrett had been fighting. She'd told him she loved him, and he'd refused to believe her. Later, they'd been at the bayou. She was on one side and he was on the other. He'd held the paintings—only they were smaller—and said, "They're mine, Molly. How can I steal what's mine?"

Her eyes flew open, as new insight swept through her. The dream-Garrett was right. Her earlier theory didn't wash at all. She was regarding the paintings as hers, and in a way, they were. But technically, Garrett owned them, since he'd bought back the plantation. And if they belonged to him, why would he need to have them copied and then switched on the sly? He could do what he wanted with them—openly. He certainly didn't need her permission. Likewise, if he'd decided to sell them and wanted copies made because they were a part of the plantation's heritage, why not just commission Krystal and pay her?

The knowledge went a long way in restoring her peace of mind. She didn't know what was going on, but she was relieved to feel that Garrett was innocent of any wrongdoing. A muffled sound from below sent a sudden chill down Molly's spine, and the fine hairs at the back of her neck stood at attention. Instantly alert and lying very still, she held her breath and listened for any other sounds. Tension coiled tighter inside her. She'd lived in the house for twelve years with the legendary presence of a ghost and never been afraid. But she was afraid now.

Something…someone was in the house. And there was no way she was going to lie there and wait for whoever it was to find her. Easing her legs over the side of the high bed, Molly fumbled for the matches. She scratched one down the sandpaper strip and was rewarded with a small blaze that wavered in the darkness. Careful to shield the flame with her hand, she carried the match to the wick. It caught at once, and she breathed a sigh of relief. The flickering light revealed that no one lurked in the corners of her room.

Carrying the lamp, she tiptoed to the door. Opening it a crack, she peeked down the hallway toward the stairs. Empty. She lifted the hurricane lamp higher and started down the steps, careful to avoid those that squeaked. As soon as she reached the main floor, she could see a shaft of weak light escaping from the half-opened door of Garrett's study. Sidling nearer, she peeked through. A powerful flashlight sat on the desk, lighting the way for a fair-haired man wearing black clothing and sneakers, who was slowly turning the dial of Garrett's safe.

Molly's heart leapt to her throat. Someone was trying to get into Garrett's safe! Who would know he had one? He didn't keep any money at the house, and the only things of great value they kept there were the paintings, which were gone, and the ruby and diamond jewelry. Which was gone. She stifled a near-hysterical laugh at the irony of it.

As she watched, the man stopped and cocked his head, as if he was aware someone was nearby. Molly ducked down the hallway out of sight. Without thinking of the folly of her move, she raced up the stairs, determined to put distance between herself and the thief. Haste made her careless, and her bare foot came down on the wrong step before she reached the landing. The loud creak made her realize just how careless she'd been.

Molly heard footsteps approaching the bottom of the stairs. She reached the second floor and closed her bedroom door—her squeaking bedroom door—behind her just before a beam of light was directed upward. Realizing that she'd made a grave error in judgment, Molly set down the lamp and opened the door a crack to see if the burglar was following.

He was.

She could see his light in the stairwell. He was creeping stealthily upward, pausing at each step, listening...waiting, fearful, perhaps, of ambush. For a moment, Molly was paralyzed, her mind racing as she wondered what to do.

Close the door.

The words came to her as clearly as if someone in the room had spoken them. Molly closed the door, thankful it didn't creak, careful not to let the catch click. She turned back to the room and leaned against the door. Her heart was beating so hard it seemed that whoever was in the house must surely hear it. Her eyes scanned the room, looking for...what? A weapon? A place to hide?

A panicked sob fought its way up her throat; she covered her mouth with her hand to hold it back. Her head whipped to the side. Was that another squeak on the stairs? Dear God, what was she going to do?

Turn out the lamp.

Of course. If he saw the lamplight beneath her door, he would know where she was. If he already didn't. Molly reached over and turned down the wick, plunging the room into total darkness. She stood still for several seconds, letting her eyes adjust to the dark and forcing herself to calm down.

Think, Molly! Think! What's your advantage? She couldn't think of a thing except that she knew he was coming. Thank goodness he hadn't caught her completely off guard. Everything else was in his favor. She was a woman—a pregnant woman—and the intruder was a man. Bigger than she was. Stronger. He wanted something, and she stood between him and whatever that something was. Molly refused to think of what he might do to her if he found her.

The house. Use the house.

The voice whispered inside her, around her. For a moment, Molly had no idea what the voice meant, and then she realized that, unlike the stranger, she knew the layout of the house. Unlike the man coming up her stairs, who needed a flashlight to see, she could find her way around in the dark. She knew where every piece of furniture was, every piece of bric-a-brac, every nook and hiding place.

She didn't have to wait here for him to find her. Moving with the quiet and care that she'd seen the barn cats use when stalking an unsuspecting mouse, Molly circled her bed and headed her soft footfalls to the door that joined her bedroom to Krystal's. Wrapping cold, numb fingers around the doorknob, she turned it.

Nothing happened. Tears of anger and frustration stung beneath her eyelids. Damn! Krystal had the door locked from the other side. Pressing her fingertips to her burning eyes, Molly forced herself to think. She needed something to push the key out with and something for it to fall on.

The newspaper! she thought exultantly. She could slide the newspaper she'd been reading earlier, beneath the door. With any luck at all, the key would fall onto the paper and she could pull it back into the room and unlock the door from this side.

What could she use to poke the key out? Molly made a quick inventory of what was in the bedroom. Nail clippers, fingernail polish, her fingernail file. That was it! She could use the file. The only problem was, that it was on the table on the other side of the bed. Holding her breath and praying that she wouldn't be caught, Molly moved as quickly as possible back around the bed. From across the hall, she heard the almost imperceptible closing of a door. The door of Garrett's room.

Please...

Her fingers groped around on the surface of the nightstand and finally found the slender metal object, which was lying on top of the newspaper. Drawing a sigh of relief, she retrieved both items, backing away from the table and around the foot of the bed. She cut the corner too sharply and bumped the bedpost with her hip. The contact made a dull thud but, to Molly, it sounded as if someone had dropped an anvil into the room. She bit back a cry of pain and moved steadily toward the doorway, her eyes straining to pick out any movement in the darkness.

When she reached the door, she got onto her knees and unfolded the paper, sliding it under the door as far as she could and still retaining enough grip to pull it back through. Then, skimming the door with her fingers, she located the keyhole and inserted the nail file, probing with care for the round end of the old-fashioned skeleton key. There was a muffled *thunk* as it fell to the floor.

Molly could have cried with relief. It had landed on the paper. Grasping the edge of the newspaper, she inched it back into her bedroom, hoping that the key was safely in the center where it was in no danger of sliding off. It was through! She gave a silent prayer of thanks when her fingers closed around the cool metal.

Rising to her knees, she felt for the keyhole once again. There was a slight grating noise when she put the key in and a click when she turned it. Why wasn't there thunder and rain to cover the noise she was making? Knowing there was no time to waste, Molly drew her feet under her and grasped the nob. At the precise instant she turned it, she heard her own door squeak open from the hallway. Her heart pounding in her throat, Molly released the door, ducked and drew herself into a ball. . . .

There was no sense fooling himself, Garrett thought as he negotiated his rental car through the storm-buffeted night. He'd missed Molly. He had told her that it was worth making the trip to New Jersey to see if he could get the financing for the crawfish venture come spring. The truth was he'd needed to put some distance between himself and her.

Time away from her hadn't done any good. He'd missed her so much that when he'd heard that the storms were approaching, he'd scheduled his flight to Dallas/Fort Worth instead of to New Orleans. It was better to add a long drive from DFW to Rambler's Rest than to wait for the weather to clear and tack on another day before seeing her.

If anyone would have told him that he would come to depend on a woman's presence, he would have called him a liar. But he had. She refilled his coffee cup without his asking. His underwear was always folded and his socks matched up. She handled the tours and dinners, freeing him to take care of the land and outbuildings. Most of all it was her quiet company he had begun to rely on. Molly had insinuated herself into his life in so many ways that it was easier to imagine losing the plantation than losing her.

That dependency had become worse since the day she'd followed him to the bayou, all wild willful woman, determined to get some answers. He'd been surprised at her uninhibited behavior as she seduced him in the lush grass growing along the water's edge. With her temper, he should have known there would be equal amounts of passion, but her actions and his response had been a revelation.

If he'd wanted her before, now she was an addiction. He found himself less eager to go to the fields. More often than not, he joined her after lunch, when she rested during the heat of the afternoon. She was warm and generous and never once asked him for a verbal commitment. He was beginning to believe he'd never be able to leave her, which was why he'd needed the week away to get his feelings and emotions into perspective.

Rain pelted his windshield as the storm got its second wind. Garrett hardly noticed. Happiness and contentment settled inside him at the knowledge that he'd soon have Molly in his arms . . . in his bed. As the car neared the circular driveway of the plantation, Garrett was aware that the time to himself hadn't worked. Nothing had changed. And, while he still refused to recognize those feelings as that fickle emotion called love, he admitted that he'd never felt about another woman the way he felt about Molly.

The wind screamed through the trees, whipping the bushes and flinging the rain against the house where it slid away in cold, gray sheets. Thank God, the storm had started up again. Lying quietly in her hiding place beneath the bed, Molly held her breath and prayed that the thunder would drown out her ragged breathing and the terrified pounding of her heart.

A bolt of lightning seared the sky. Peeking out from behind the dust ruffle, Molly saw the intruder's sneaker-clad feet as he rounded the foot of the bed and approached the door that led to Krystal's room. Molly realized that she must have pushed on the door when she rolled away because it was standing three-quarters of the way open.

With the rays of the flashlight preceding him, the stranger advanced slowly, quietly. Reaching the door, he flashed the light into the corners of Krystal's room, and then, as if he suddenly realized that the far door led to the hall, he pivoted and headed back through Molly's room the way he'd come. Why? she asked herself.

Carefully, she eased out from beneath the bed. Listening... listening. The only sound she heard was her heart beating. She forced herself to breathe through her mouth. She'd read somewhere that it made less noise than breathing through the nose.

Moving with the silence of a wraith, she crossed Krystal's room and gently turned the knob of her hall door, risking a peek to see if her pursuer was anywhere nearby. The wide passageway was empty and fairly dark, but she did see his flashlight, a square, powerful-looking instrument, that gave off a strong beam of light, sitting near the top of the stairs.

Where was he, and why had he abandoned his only source of light? She was considering the possibility of sneaking across the hall and going from room to room until she reached the one nearest the stairs, when she realized what he was doing.

He must suspect that whoever had opened the connecting doorway had sneaked from Krystal's room into one of the four rooms opposite. Like her, the intruder was using the darkness to his advantage, hiding. He'd left the flashlight near the stairs so that he could see her if she tried to make a break for freedom.

What should she do? Molly weighed her options carefully. He could be anywhere. She was quick; he was strong. She had navigated the stairs hundreds of times and knew the height of the steps and their feel. It wouldn't matter if they squeaked on the way down; he could take the stairs two at a time. She was carrying a baby that she wanted to bring safely into the world, and she couldn't do that if he found her. The thought of Garrett's baby was the decisive factor. She was going to make a run for it.

A sound, like thousands of golf balls falling, pelted the roof. Without waiting for her courage to falter, Molly flung open the door and raced down the hall. The stairs looked an eternity away. She zeroed in on them, looking neither to the right nor left, her bare feet hardly touching the smooth wood floor as she sped toward the only hope in sight.

Suddenly from behind her, she heard the heavy pounding of feet as her assailant gave chase. Panic rose in waves as she calculated the nearness of safety. There was only the length of one room to go and then the expanse of the double doors that led to the side balcony. Molly's foot had actually reached out to take the first step when she felt hard hands grab the voluminous fabric of her gown and jerk her backward into a hard, masculine body.

She screamed.

Garrett, who had just made a wild dash to escape the thundering hail, heard the scream even over the sound of the demoniacal wind. Molly! He thrust his key in the lock and turned it and the knob simultaneously. The wind grabbed the door from his hand, propelling him into the wide lower hall.

The light drew his attention to the top of the stairs. For an instant, Garrett's heart stopped. Then it shuddered and began to gallop in fear. Molly and a man were struggling. His hands were wrapped around her throat. She clawed at his wrists, trying to free herself. Garrett started up the stairs, her name on his lips. . . .

The man's thumbs pressed tighter, harder. Molly fought against an overwhelming darkness. Her assailant's face wavered before her eyes as they drifted closed. She thought she heard Garrett's voice call her name and gladly gave herself over to the floating sensation that would take her to him.

Outside, the wind howled like a banshee. The latch of the gallery doors gave way, twisting one from its hinges. They banged against the inner walls, letting sheets of icy rain inside. Glass panes shattered to the floor.

Enveloped in the cold wind, hardly able to stand, Molly felt her captor's grip on her throat loosen. Above the wind, there was a hoarse masculine cry followed by the sounds of a body falling down the stairs. Miraculously free, Molly fell to her knees, grabbing the railing for a lifeline. He was gone. Thank God. The wind was gone, too; there was nothing but the sound of rain against the roof. The silence was almost deafening after the noise of the storm. Rolling onto her back, she drew harsh, gasping drafts of air through her burning throat.

Then, unbelievably, she heard the heavy thud of feet as someone ran up the stairs. Tears of exhaustion trickled from the corners of her closed eyes. Please, God, no, she thought. Enough.

Strong arms scooped her against a hard, warm chest and a familiar masculine scent filled her nostrils. Hot lips rained frantic kisses over her face. A man's voice, thickened with tears, murmured her name.

Molly made the supreme effort and forced her leaden eyelids upward.

"Garrett," she breathed, her voice soft with wonder. She tried to raise a hand to touch him, wanted to tell him she was all right now that he was there, but all she could do was whisper his name once more before she closed her eyes, knowing that she was safe in his arms.

Chapter Twelve

When Molly woke up, the sun was shining through the window straight into her eyes. She lifted a weary hand to shield them from the shimmering brightness and realized that the storm was over. She also realized that the morning sun didn't come through her bedroom window. For a second, she was disoriented. Wincing when she lifted her head, she looked around. She was in Garrett's room.

Memories, like the wind sweeping through the doors the night before, whirled through her mind: the storm raging outside while she hid from the stranger; struggling with him on the stairs the same way Silvie had struggled with Henri so long ago; knowing, as Silvie had, that she was going to be thrown down into the terrible darkness waiting for her and her unborn baby....

A delinquent frisson of fear scampered down Molly's spine, and her hands went to her still-flat stomach where Garrett's baby rested, snug and safe. A breeze, a remnant from the storm, drifted through the open window and reminded her of the surprising, typhoon-force rush of wind that had loosened the interloper's hands from her neck. She could still hear the sound of him falling down the stairs, could still remember her relief and Garrett, pale and grim-faced, holding her close.

She'd fainted, but had come around later, after Garrett had put her in his bed and tied up the unconscious burglar. When the police arrived, he refused to let them see her, promising that she would talk with them today. He'd wanted to take her to a doctor, but she'd convinced him that she was fine. And she was, except for some aching muscles...and hunger that gnawed at her.

A sound at the door drew Molly's attention. Shiloh entered the room, concern in her deep-blue eyes. "Good morning," she said as she approached the bed.

Molly thought again what a beautiful woman Shiloh was. Short and built on a dainty scale, she nonetheless possessed a curvaceous body that made those less fortunate green with envy. Her hair, lighter than Garrett's, was cut to the curve of her jaw. The jagged look of the bangs which were brushed to one side, and the wispy, uneven strands that hugged her cheeks— longer on one side than the other—looked as if her hairdresser had been careless. However, Molly knew her sister-in-law paid up to a hundred dollars for the haircut that made her look closer to eighteen than to the thirty she was.

"Hello, yourself," Molly said, smiling in genuine pleasure. "What are you doing here?"

"Lucky for you, I just happened to be in Dallas visiting one of my old sorority sisters. Garrett tracked me down and asked me to drive over and stay with you, and ta da! Here I am." Shiloh's eyes twinkled with mischief. "I got here about one in the morning, during all the excitement, and you were out like a light."

Molly tried to smile. "It was . . . quite a night."

"From what I hear, that's putting it mildly." Shiloh sat down on the edge of the bed. "I guess you figured out that a tornado touched down nearby."

"A tornado?"

Shiloh nodded. "The roof of the barn is gone, and the big tree down near the bayou is nowhere to be found."

Molly's first thought was of the livestock. "Are the horses all right?"

"They're fine. The buckskin has a cut on his hip and they're both pretty skittish, but they're fine. Garrett sent them to the Reynolds's."

Molly drew a sigh of relief. "You say the big tree is gone?"

"Nothing left but a hole you could set the bathroom in."

The barn had been sturdily built at least fifty years before, and the live oak was a hundred if it was a day. It was hard to fathom that things which seemed so permanent could be taken away in the space of a heartbeat. Like life. And love. It made Molly want to gather all the good things close and hoard them. "Unbelievable."

"I know," Shiloh said, pushing back an unruly lock of Molly's hair. "How are you feeling?"

Shiloh's tenderness was Molly's undoing. "I'm fine," Molly said tremulously and promptly burst into tears. The stress of the last month combined with her pregnancy, the uncertainty over what was going to happen between her and Garrett, and the fact that someone had tried to kill her, had drained her emotional reserves.

Shiloh gathered her close and held her while she cried, held her until the harsh sobs subsided to gentle hiccups. Then she brought Molly a cool washcloth to wipe away the ravages of her tears.

Molly dabbed at her still-leaking eyes and sniffed. "I'm sorry. I don't know what's the matter with me. I need to get up and fix Garrett's breakfast instead of lying here feeling sorry for myself."

Shiloh met Molly's gaze head-on. "And here I was, thinking we'd made a major breakthrough."

"What?"

"Don't you ever get tired?" Shiloh asked with a gentle smile.

"Of what?"

"Being strong all the time. You're such a gutsy woman, Molly. I remember when you were just a kid, how you stood up to your mother and told her how you disapproved of what she was doing. And how you never let what happened around you affect your actions. You were always so in control of your feelings. No matter what happened, you seemed to take it in stride. You just got up and went on with your life. I used to wonder how you did it."

Molly stared at Shiloh in disbelief, yet knew that what she was saying was true. Molly's eyes glazed over again. She needed to tell someone how she felt, and at the moment, Garrett's sister seemed like the ideal person.

"It's hard to explain," Molly began. "You're right. But for as long as I can remember, my life was in chaos in one way or another. The only consistencies were the routines I created. So I was the one who cooked and cleaned and picked up. I did it because I wanted my life to be normal, like everyone else's."

"I remember feeling the same way," Shiloh said.

"You!"

"My parents were divorced, too—remember?"

How could she have forgotten? Molly smiled apologetically. "I think the worst part for me, was the loneliness. Did you know that I used to talk to Silvie back then? Actually," she said, an embarrassed look entering her eyes, "I still do. There was no one else to confide in, and I was so mortified over the way Mom and Krystal acted. I wanted desperately not to be like them."

"You aren't like either of them," Shiloh told her. "Trust me."

"Thanks," Molly said with a grim smile. "That's the nicest thing anyone's ever said to me."

"You're welcome," Shiloh said. "Well, are you going to give up this martyr complex now that you have Garrett to love you and take care of you?"

Molly looked stunned. "I married Garrett because I loved him, but Garrett doesn't love me. He married me because I care for the plantation as much as he does."

Shiloh lifted delicate, arched eyebrows and wrinkled her nose in disdain. "That's what he told me, too, but I told him he was fooling himself."

Molly was afraid to believe what she was hearing. "Do you mean—"

"That Garrett is in love with you? Yeah." Shiloh winked. "But I'm not sure the jerk knows it yet. Garrett's never had a woman he could count on until you." She patted Molly's hand and stood. "You just hang in there and stop worrying. He'll come around and tell you sooner or later."

Molly's mind spun with possibilities. "But . . . how can I trust him if he says he loves me?"

It was Shiloh's turn to look surprised. "Why shouldn't you believe him? My brother is a lot of things, but he isn't a liar."

"Believe what you want . . ." Memory of Garrett's words when he refused to tell her his side of the story about his breakup with Krystal drifted through her mind. "But, Krystal—"

Shiloh's eyes grew stormy with anger. "Krystal? Let me tell you about Krystal. She broke Garrett's heart."

Molly's mouth fell open in surprise. "But she said—"

Shiloh's eyes widened. "I see. She told you it was the other way around?"

Molly nodded. "She said that Garrett slept with her best friend."

"Oh, really?" Shiloh's voice dripped sarcasm. "Would you like to know what really happened?"

"Please," Molly whispered.

"I was dating Don Ramsay. He'd even asked me to marry him. Garrett went out to the barn one evening and found Don and Krystal together in the haymow. Garrett's a smart guy, and in their state of dress—or undress—he figured they weren't looking for the proverbial needle in the haystack."

She threaded her slender fingers through her hair and looked at Molly apologetically. "I'm sorry. I don't mean to put Krys down, but when it comes to clearing Garrett's name—"

"It's all right," Molly said, filled with a sense of relief that Garrett was innocent of Krystal's claims. "And what happened with you and Don?"

"Don thought he'd fallen for Krystal until Garrett made him see reason. Don came to me and said he was sorry, but I couldn't forgive him. Not then. Not ever. If you'll remember I went back to Tennessee early. That's why."

"Do you still love him?"

Shiloh shook her head. "I'm not sure I ever really did. I got over the hurt, but it was just one more reason for me to steer clear of marriage."

"Don't give up on love, Shiloh. It's out there. Didn't you just tell me that Garrett loved me? We just have to look longer and harder to find the real thing."

Shiloh sighed. "Maybe you're right." She straightened her shoulders, visibly trying to put the memories aside. "Enough of that. I'm here to take care of you. I'm going downstairs to fix you some of my world-renowned crepes. You rest."

"But what about Garrett's breakfast?"

"Garrett is a big boy. If he gets hungry, he knows how to pour cereal from a box. I personally feel you're entitled to a few tears and a day in bed after your ordeal last night. Of course," Shiloh continued tongue-in-cheek, "that's just my opinion. You think about it, and I'll be back in a jiffy."

Molly watched Shiloh go, thankful that Garrett had called her.

After she'd eaten her strawberry-and-whipped-creme-filled crepes, Molly took a long hot bath and dressed in a casual skirt and scoop-necked knit shirt, preparing to face the day and the police. Garrett hadn't put in an appearance all morning, and Molly was starting to feel uneasy about how to greet him. Had she just imagined the tenderness in his voice and the kisses he'd given her before she'd lost consciousness?

She dabbed foundation on the dark-purple bruise at the hollow of her throat. It didn't help much. Taking a tissue from the box, she wiped the makeup away and draped a scarf around her neck instead. She tried to ignore the trembling of her hands and the whisperings inside her that reminded her that she'd almost been killed.

A knock sounded at her door, and Shiloh poked her head in. "The police are here. Garrett wanted me to come get you."

"Thanks." Drawing in a deep breath, Molly rose from the vanity stool and started downstairs. There was a terrible moment as she reached the spot where the struggle had taken place, but, then, seeing the mangled gallery doors, the feeling of unease passed, and she felt a sense of gratitude for the renegade wind. The house, as she'd known it would, had survived. So had she.

And so, she vowed, would her marriage.

She'd always known why the house was important to her, but after talking with Shiloh, she understood why it was so important to Garrett. As Shiloh said, her parents were divorced, too. The house had been Garrett's home, his security, as it had become hers.

There were three men in Garrett's study: a young uniformed policeman, an older, gruff-looking detective and Garrett, who sat behind his desk, a brooding look on his face. He stood when she entered the room, made the introductions, and led her to a chair across the desk from his. Instead of returning to his own seat, he settled himself on a corner of the desk, one booted foot swinging back and forth.

"Can you tell us what happened, Mrs. Rambler?" the detective, named Cal Simmons, asked.

As simply as she could, Molly related what had happened, starting with her waking up and hearing someone in the house. Concentrating on the policeman's questions, she didn't notice the tightening of Garrett's lips when she told about hiding under the bed, or the agony in his eyes when she described her struggle with the thief. Without realizing it, her hand crept to her throat as she related the scene in minute detail. The sound of a muffled curse from Garrett drew everyone's attention.

His gaze was glued to the bruises on her neck. Seeing the root of Garrett's distress, the policeman in uniform whistled in surprise.

"I know it was a harrowing experience for you, Mrs. Rambler, but you can rest easy knowing that we do have your sister's husband in custody."

"My sister's husband?" Molly echoed. She glanced at the policeman for an explanation.

"It might be easier if you tell her, Mr. Rambler," the older man said.

Garrett nodded but didn't speak. Standing, he went to the window and looked at the limb-and-debris-strewn yard, kneading the muscles at the back of his neck. "The man who... tried to... rob us was Krystal's husband."

"Freddy!" Molly couldn't hide her surprise. "What's he doing here? Krystal left him in Greece."

Garrett turned, a look of determination on his face. "No. She didn't leave him in Greece. As a matter of fact, she didn't leave him at all. They were in this together."

Molly looked from Garrett to the detective and back again. "In what, together?"

"The theft of the paintings and the attempted theft of the jewelry," Cal Simmons interjected.

Molly held up her hands. "Wait. I'm lost."

"Krystal lied to you, Molly," Garrett said, taking up the story again. "She and Freddy never split up. They were broke, though, so they started working on a way they could get their hands on some easy money. She found out that you were barely making it, so she couldn't hit you up for anything.

"Then she accidentally ran into Spiro in Greece, got next to him solely for the purpose of finding out if there was anything of value at the plantation when he was married to Liz. He let it slip that the paintings were still here. She said that she'd even asked you about them to make sure. You corroborated Spiro's story."

Molly remembered the telephone call from Krystal on the day Mac Henning had given her the ultimatum about the loan.

"Krystal spent the next few weeks trying to get the money together to fly back. When she found out we were married, she was afraid that I'd mess up her plans. So, she cooked up the story about leaving Freddy—which we bought, to a degree—and set out copying the paintings, which she did in record time because Landseer's and Bonheur's styles are remarkably similar.''

"Krystal switched the paintings?"

Garrett nodded.

Oh, Krystal... Krystal... "When?"

"When you were at the doctor's. She passed the originals on to Freddy the day you saw them at the bayou. When I told her to get out, she probably jumped for joy. My asking her to leave cast much less suspicion on her than if she'd just disappeared.''

Molly mulled over what she'd just learned. There were still many unanswered questions. "If they already had the paintings, why was Freddy trying to break into your safe?"

"Krystal heard me mention the jewelry when we were talking about how we were going to finance the crawfish farm. When they got to Shreveport, she told Freddy, who obviously got greedy. He told her he was going to contact someone he knew in Dallas, but came back down here instead. He watched the place for a few days and figured out that I was gone. What he didn't know was that I had the jewelry. He decided that last night was the perfect time, since any noise he made would be covered by the storm. He thought he could get in and out without anyone being the wiser. Then, the rain stopped and messed up all his plans.''

"So he had to try and kill me." She said the words in a voice totally devoid of emotion.

Garrett didn't say anything.

Molly shivered.

"Of course, he'll come to trial, ma'am," Detective Simmons said. "But we need to know if you plan to press charges against your sister. She is an accessory."

Press charges against Krystal? Molly gripped the arms of the chair to stop the spinning of the room. How could she send her own flesh and blood to jail?

She looked at the policeman. "Where is she now?"

"They picked her up in Shreveport, and we're holding her in Thibodaux. She swears that she knew nothing about her husband's plans to rob the house. She was pretty distraught when she found out he'd tried to hurt you."

Garrett plunged his hands in his pockets; his eyes met Molly's. "It's your call."

"What about you?" she asked. "Are you pressing charges over the paintings?"

He shook his head. "The police found them in Krystal's motel room. I'll get them back."

"Then, no," Molly said to the two policemen. "I won't press charges against my sister—under one condition." From the corner of her eyes, Molly saw Garrett turn away.

"What's that, ma'am?"

"That she get professional help."

Detective Simmons smiled crookedly. "I'll see what I can do." The two men stood and shook hands with both Garrett and Molly.

At the door, the older policeman turned. "Just one more thing, Mrs. Rambler."

"Yes?"

"Freddy said to tell you that you were the strongest woman he'd ever come up against."

"I beg your pardon?" Molly said with a frown.

"When you pushed him down the stairs."

"I'm sorry, officer, but I don't know what you mean. Freddy was choking me. I was almost unconscious when the doors blew open. I didn't push him. If anything, the force of the wind caused him to lose his hold on me." Molly shrugged. "It must have made him lose his balance."

"No ma'am," the younger policeman piped in. "He said he distinctly felt two hands push him down the stairs."

"It was probably just the excitement," Molly said, not knowing what to say.

"Yeah, probably," Simmons agreed. "So long, Mrs. Rambler. Someone will be in touch."

Garrett ushered them from the room, and Molly wandered out onto the back gallery, her forehead wrinkled in perplexity. The sound of masculine voices was a faraway drone as she pondered the policeman's story. Surely she hadn't had the strength or the presence of mind to shove Freddy away and cause him to fall down the stairs.

"Are you all right?"

The sound of Garrett's voice jarred her thoughts back to the present. He looked big and powerful and...concerned, she thought, her heart fluttering inside her chest. She nodded. "A little tired."

"I was going to check out some of the damage. Want to come?"

"Yes," Molly said, desperate to get some normalcy back in her life.

Garrett crossed the porch and took her hand. Very gently he pushed aside the scarf and looked at the bruises marring the creamy perfection of her throat. Unexpectedly, he bent and pressed his mouth to the them. Then, he crushed her in his arms and held her close.

"All for nothing," he said in her ear. "You were almost killed for a bunch of paste."

Molly drew back to look at him. "What?"

Garrett's mouth twisted. "We thought we had a good idea, trying to use the ruby jewels to finance the crawfish farm. But somebody beat us to it."

"What are you talking about?"

"The jewelry isn't real, Molly. The guy who wanted to buy it took it to have it appraised and found out the gems were paste." He laughed humorlessly. "It was pretty damned embarrassing, not to mention shocking. Some other Rambler probably lost the real ones gambling and had the fakes made to keep up appearances."

"No wonder Liz let Jon have them," Molly said with a smile.

Garrett nodded, a real smile curving his own lips. "She probably had them appraised herself."

"Did you ever think the day would come when we could laugh about what happened between Jon and Liz?" Molly asked.

"No." Garrett looked into her eyes, and the smile in his faded. He took her face between his palms and looked at her with his heart in his eyes. "I thought I'd die when I heard you scream," he confessed in an emotion-roughened voice.

Molly didn't answer. She couldn't. All she could do was try and hold back the tears of happiness springing up inside her.

"When I saw you with him on the stairs..." His voice trailed away.

"I'm all right," she said reaching up and placing her hand against his cheek. "It was terrible, but—"

"I love you, Molly."

"—I'll— What did you say?" She looked up at him, her green eyes dark with emotion.

"I said I love you. I didn't think I'd ever fall in love." One corner of his finely-shaped lips lifted. "Especially not with you. I fought it. I didn't want to. I—"

Molly lifted her hand and covered his mouth with her fingers. "I get the picture."

Garrett kissed her fingers, and Molly slid her arms around his neck. "You're sure? I mean you don't have to say it, if—"

"I'm sure."

"I mean, I am Liz's daughter. And Krystal's sister. And—"

Garrett's mouth swooped down and took hers with a bruising kiss that lasted until they were both breathless. He rested his forehead against hers. "I get the picture."

"Mmm," Molly agreed. "It's happy."

"What?"

"The picture. Of our future. Just like Nate's and Lisette's."

Smiling indulgently, a smile that reminded Molly of the smiles her father gave Veronica, Garrett draped his arm around her shoulders, and together they crossed the porch to the backyard. Molly stared up at him, adoring his strong profile.

"When did you know?" she asked, skipping along in the wet grass to keep up with him.

Garrett stopped and looked at her, love in his eyes. "I suspected for a long time, but knew it the moment I saw you at the top of the stairs and thought I was losing you."

A bird sang sweetly in a nearby tree, and a gentle breeze caressed her cheeks. Molly traced the shape of his upper lip with her fingertip. "I've loved you forever. Maybe longer."

"What?"

She grinned impishly and shrugged. "Well, since I was fourteen, anyway."

"That's a long time to care for someone when you aren't sure they'll ever care for you," Garrett said, as if the thought was beyond his comprehension.

All pretense of humor fled from Molly's face. "When you love someone," she said seriously, "you don't have any choice about when it comes or how long it lasts."

Garrett looked at her as if he couldn't believe she was real. "I'm beginning to see that."

Standing on tiptoe, Molly pressed her mouth to his.

"To hell with checking the damages," Garrett said on a sigh. He scooped her up in his arms and started back toward the house.

"You'll never make it," she teased, gauging the distance.

"Oh, ye of little faith."

"You're carrying two, don't forget."

"How could I?"

"Listen, Garrett!"

He stopped. "What?"

"Do you hear it? It sounds like Silvie's chimes."

Garrett lowered her to the ground and listened, trying to locate the sound. "There they are," he told her pointing to a nearby tree.

Approaching the spot, Molly shielded her eyes against the brilliant brightness of the summer sun. Sure enough, there, in the low branches of an oak, hung the tangled wind chimes, tinkling softly.

"The storm blew them down," Garrett said.

"Do you think we can get them?"

He shook his head. "I doubt we can without ruining them. We'll have to get some more."

The thought was sad somehow. For no apparent reason, the policeman's words filtered through her mind. "What do you think about what Detective Simmons said about me pushing Freddy?"

Garrett took her hand and, pulling her along behind him, started walking again.

"Did you?" Garrett asked, with an inquisitive lift of one eyebrow. "If you did, remind me to treat you real nice."

Molly skipped ahead of him. Walking backwards, she poked him in the chest with her index finger. "You'd better be nice to me, and no, I did not push him."

"Well, if you didn't, who do you think did?"

Molly recalled the voice she'd heard when she was so afraid. The voice that had given her specific instructions on what to do.

She stopped dead in her tracks, and Garrett almost mowed her down. He gripped her shoulders. "What is it?"

"Silvie," Molly said, awe in her voice. "It was Silvie."

"Molly..."

"The legend says that Silvie will haunt the house until she can do something—help someone—to make amends for not helping Lisette."

Garrett grinned. "I'd better call Pineville and tell them to reserve a bed for you next to Aunt Lisbet's."

Molly grabbed his shirt and shook him. "Listen." Her eyes were luminous with belief. "It was almost like history repeating itself. Silvie was pregnant. She was struggling on the stairs with Henri when Lisette came to her rescue. Lisette almost got killed because Silvie wouldn't help her. So Silvie haunted the house, waiting for the right time, the right circumstance."

"And?"

"And I'm pregnant. I was fighting Freddy in the same spot where Lisette and Henri struggled. But this time, Silvie did help."

"Are you saying that you think that Silvie pushed Freddy?" Garrett asked incredulously.

Molly looked up at him, her face a study in seriousness. The sun gilded her eyelashes and teased the gold highlights from her hair. "What other explanation is there?"

Not a cloud marred the azure blue of the sky. Not a breath of wind was blowing, yet suddenly, a capricious breeze whirled around them. It spun away, flitting through the oak tree a few yards away, dancing through the wind chimes and sending the tiny bells into silvery song. And high above the tinkling bells came the teasing sound of a silvery song. And high above the tinkling bells came the teasing sound of a young girl's laughter.

*   *   *   *   *

Silhouette Special Edition

COMING NEXT MONTH

#619 THE GIRL MOST LIKELY TO—Tracy Sinclair
Kate Beaumont was desperate for a man—even if she had to hire one!—for her high school reunion. And after seeing the shy, sexy scientist in distress, Garrett Richmond gladly offered his masculine services...

#620 NO PLACE TO HIDE—Celeste Hamilton
Urban refugee Carly Savoy thought she had found safety in her secluded mountain retreat—until mysterious Ben Jamison shattered her sanctuary and threatened to unravel her innermost secrets.

#621 ALL WE KNOW OF HEAVEN—Phyllis Halldorson
After seven agonizing years of grief and regret, Michaela Tanner forced herself to assume the worst about her P.O.W. husband, Heath. But on the eve of her second marriage, Heath's presence was more than mere memory...

#622 PETTICOAT LAWYER—Kate Meriwether
Camille Clark rallied all the toughness she could muster to face police officer Pike Barrett in court. But Pike, detecting softness beneath the stunning attorney's brittle sophistication, was determined not to remain her adversary for long!

#623 FREEDOM'S JUST ANOTHER WORD—Jennifer Mikels
The only thing conservative Joshua Fitzhugh shared with free-spirited Allison Gentry was his boardinghouse bathroom. But in his search for a "suitable" mate, the sensible professor was hopelessly sidetracked by his offbeat neighbor!

#624 OLD ENOUGH TO KNOW BETTER—Pamela Toth
One decade after escaping a domestic dead end, Maureen Fletcher remained blissfully single. Then her heart was hooked by handsome Bailey McGuire—but, at her age, could she handle ready-made motherhood?

AVAILABLE THIS MONTH:

COMING SOON...

For years Harlequin and Silhouette novels
have been taking readers places—but only in
their imaginations.

This fall look for PASSPORT TO ROMANCE,
a promotion that could take you around the
corner or around the world!

Watch for it in September!

★